COLLECTION 4

Goosebumps available now:

Look out for:

COLLECTION 4

The Haunted Mask
Piano Lessons Can Be Murder
Be Careful What You Wish For

R.L. Stine

Hippo

Scholastic Children's Books,
Commonwealth House, 1–19 New Oxford Street, London WC1A 1NU, UK
a division of Scholastic Ltd
London ~ New York ~ Toronto ~ Sydney ~ Auckland

First published in this edition by Scholastic Ltd, 1996

The Haunted Mask
Piano Lessons Can Be Murder
Be Careful What You Wish For
First published in the USA by Scholastic Inc., 1993
First published in the UK by Scholastic Ltd, 1994

ISBN 0 590 13740 9

Typeset by Contour Typesetters, Southall, London
Printed by Cox & Wyman Ltd, Reading, Berks

10 9 8 7 6 5

CONTENTS

The Haunted Mask

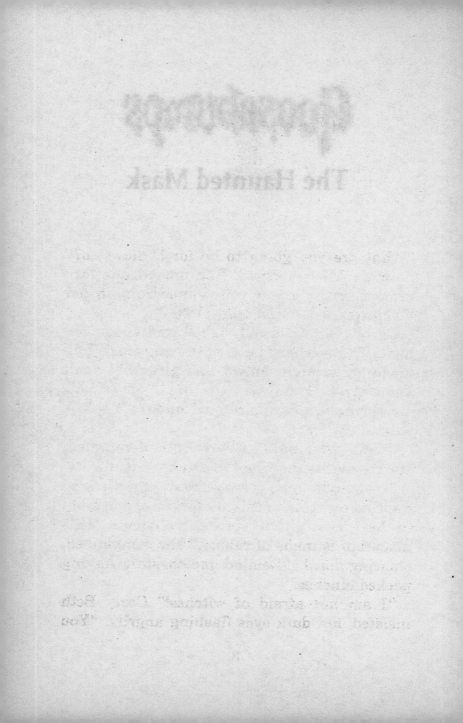

"What are you going to be for Hallowe'en?" Sabrina Mason asked. She moved her fork around in the bright yellow macaroni on her lunch tray, but didn't take a bite.

Carly Beth Caldwell sighed and shook her head. The overhead light on the canteen ceiling made her straight brown hair gleam. "I don't know. A witch, maybe."

Sabrina's mouth dropped open. "You? A witch?"

"Well, why not?" Carly Beth demanded, staring across the long table at her friend.

"I thought you were afraid of witches," Sabrina replied. She raised a forkful of macaroni to her mouth and started to chew. "This macaroni is made of rubber," she complained, chewing hard. "Remind me to start having packed lunches."

"I am *not* afraid of witches!" Carly Beth insisted, her dark eyes flashing angrily. "You

3

just think I'm a big scaredy-cat, don't you?"

Sabrina giggled. "Yes." She flipped her black ponytail behind her shoulders with a quick toss of her head. "Hey, don't eat the macaroni. Really, Carly Beth. It's gross." She reached across the table to keep Carly Beth from raising her fork.

"But I'm *starving*!" Carly Beth complained.

The canteen grew crowded and noisy. At the next table, a group of fifth-grade boys were tossing a half-full milk carton back and forth. Carly Beth saw Chuck Greene fold a slice of swiss roll up and shove the whole sticky thing in his mouth.

"Yuck!" She made a disgusted face at him. Then she turned back to Sabrina. "I am *not* a scaredy-cat, Sabrina. Just because everyone picks on me and—"

"Carly Beth, what about last week? Remember? At my house?" Sabrina ripped open a bag of tortilla chips and offered some across the table to her friend.

"You mean the ghost thing?" Carly Beth replied, frowning. "That was really stupid."

"But you believed it," Sabrina said with a mouthful of crisps. "You really believed my attic was haunted. You should have seen the look on your face when the ceiling started to creak, and we heard the footsteps up there."

4

"That was so cruel," Carly Beth complained, rolling her eyes.

"Then when you heard footsteps coming down the stairs, your face went all white and you screamed," Sabrina recalled. "It was only Chuck and Steve."

"You *know* I'm afraid of ghosts," Carly Beth said, blushing.

"And snakes and insects and loud noises and dark rooms and—and witches!" Sabrina declared.

"I don't see why you have to make fun of me," Carly Beth pouted. She shoved her lunch tray away. "I don't see why everyone always thinks it's so much fun to try to scare me. Even you, my best friend."

"I'm sorry," Sabrina said sincerely. She reached across the table and squeezed Carly Beth's wrist reassuringly. "You're just so easy to scare. It's hard to resist. Here. Want some more crisps?" She shoved the bag towards Carly Beth.

"Maybe I'll scare *you* some day," Carly Beth threatened.

Her friend laughed. "No way!"

Carly Beth continued to pout. She was eleven. But she was tiny. And with her round face and short stub of a nose (which she hated and wished would grow longer), she looked much younger.

Sabrina, on the other hand, was tall, dark, and sophisticated-looking. She had straight black

5

hair tied behind her head in a ponytail, and enormous, dark eyes. Everyone who saw them together assumed that Sabrina was twelve or thirteen. But, actually, Carly Beth was a month older than her friend.

"Maybe I won't be a witch," Carly Beth said thoughtfully, resting her chin on her hands. "Maybe I'll be a disgusting monster with hanging eyeballs and green slime dripping down my face and—"

A loud crash made Carly Beth scream.

It took her a few seconds to realize that it was just a lunch tray hitting the floor. She turned to see Gabe Moser, his face bright red, drop to his knees and start scooping his lunch off the floor. The canteen rang out with cheers and applause.

Carly Beth hunched down in her seat, embarrassed that she had screamed.

Her breathing had just returned to normal when a strong hand grabbed her shoulder from behind.

Carly Beth's shriek echoed through the room.

She heard laughter. At another table, someone yelled, "Way to go, Steve!"

She whipped her head around to see her friend Steve Boswell standing behind her, a mischievous grin on his face. "Gotcha," he said, letting go of her shoulder.

Steve pulled out the chair next to Carly Beth's and lowered himself over its back. His best friend, Chuck Greene, slammed his bookbag onto the table and then sat down next to Sabrina.

Steve and Chuck looked so much alike, they could have been brothers. Both were tall and thin, with straight brown hair, which they usually hid under baseball caps. Both had dark brown eyes and goofy grins. Both wore faded jeans and dark-coloured, long-sleeved T-shirts.

And both of them loved scaring Carly Beth. They loved to startle her, to make her jump and shriek.

7

They spent hours dreaming up new ways to frighten her.

She vowed every time that she would never—*ever*—fall for one of their stupid tricks again.

But so far, they had won every time.

Carly Beth always threatened to pay them back. But in all the time they'd been friends, she hadn't been able to think of anything good enough.

Chuck reached for the few remaining crisps in Sabrina's bag. She playfully slapped his hand away. "Get your own."

Steve held a crinkled package of aluminium foil under Carly Beth's nose. "Want a sandwich? I don't want it."

Carly Beth sniffed it suspiciously. "What kind is it? I'm *starving*!"

"It's a turkey sandwich. Here," Steve said, handing it to Carly Beth. "It's too dry. My mum forgot the salad cream. You want it?"

"Yeah, sure. Thanks!" Carly Beth exclaimed. She took the sandwich from him and peeled back the aluminium foil. Then she took a big bite of the sandwich.

As she started to chew, she realized that both Steve and Chuck were staring at her with big grins on their faces.

Something tasted funny. Kind of sticky and sour.

Carly Beth stopped chewing.

8

Chuck and Steve were laughing now. Sabrina looked confused.

Carly Beth uttered a disgusted groan and spat the chewed-up mouthful of sandwich into a napkin. Then she pulled the bread apart—and saw a big brown worm resting on top of the turkey.

"Ohh!" With a moan, she covered her face with her hands.

The room erupted with laughter. Cruel laughter.

"I ate a worm. I—I'm going to be sick!" Carly Beth groaned. She jumped to her feet and stared angrily at Steve. "How *could* you?" she demanded. "It isn't funny. It's—it's—"

"It isn't a real worm," Chuck said. Steve was laughing too hard to talk.

"Huh?" Carly Beth gazed down at it and felt a wave of nausea rise up from her stomach.

"It isn't real. It's rubber. Pick it up," Chuck urged.

Carly Beth hesitated.

Kids all through the vast room were whispering and pointing at her. And laughing.

"Go ahead. It isn't real. Pick it up," Chuck said, grinning.

Carly Beth reached down with two fingers and reluctantly picked the brown worm from the sandwich. It felt warm and sticky.

"Gotcha again!" Chuck said with a laugh.

It *was* real! A real worm!

With a horrified cry, Carly Beth tossed the worm at Chuck, who was laughing wildly. Then she leapt away from the table, knocking the chair over. As the chair clattered noisily against the hard floor, Carly Beth covered her mouth and ran gagging from the lunchroom.

I can still taste it! she thought.

I can still taste the worm in my mouth!

I'll pay them back for this, Carly Beth thought bitterly as she ran.

I'll pay them back. I really will.

As she pushed through the double doors and hurtled towards the girls' cloakroom, the cruel laughter followed her across the hall.·

After school, Carly Beth hurried through the corridors without talking to anyone. She heard kids laughing and whispering. She *knew* they were laughing at her.

Word had spread all over school that Carly Beth Caldwell had eaten a worm at lunch.

Carly Beth, the scaredy-cat. Carly Beth, who was frightened of her own shadow. Carly Beth, who was so easy to trick.

Chuck and Steve had sneaked a real worm, a fat brown worm, into a sandwich. And Carly Beth had taken a big bite.

What a jerk!

Carly Beth ran all the way home, three long blocks. Her anger grew with every stop.

How could they do that to me? They're supposed to be my friends!

Why do they think it's so funny to scare me?

She burst into the house, breathing hard. "Anybody home?" she called, stopping in the hallway and leaning against the banister to catch her breath.

Her mother hurried out from the kitchen. "Carly Beth! Hi! What's wrong?"

"I ran all the way," Carly Beth told her, pulling off her blue windcheater.

"Why?" Mrs Caldwell asked.

"Just felt like it," Carly Beth replied moodily.

Her mother took Carly Beth's windcheater and hung it in the hall cupboard for her. Then she brushed a hand affectionately through Carly Beth's soft brown hair. "Where'd you get the straight hair?" she muttered. Her mother was always saying that.

We don't look like mother and daughter at all, Carly Beth realized. Her mother was a tall, chubby woman with thick curls of coppery hair, and lively grey-green eyes. She was extremely energetic, seldom stood still, and talked as rapidly as she moved.

Today she was wearing a paint-stained grey sweatshirt over black Lycra tights. "Why so grumpy?" Mrs Caldwell asked. "Anything you'd care to talk about?"

Carly Beth shook her head. "Not really." She didn't feel like telling her mother that she had become the laughing-stock of Walnut Avenue Middle School.

"Come here. I have something to show you,"

12

Mrs Caldwell said, tugging Carly Beth towards the living room.

"I—I'm really not in the mood, Mum," Carly Beth told her, hanging back. "I just—"

"Come *on!*" her mother insisted, and pulled her across the hallway. Carly Beth always found it impossible to argue with her mother. She was like a hurricane, sweeping everything in her direction.

"Look!" Mrs Caldwell declared, grinning and gesturing to the mantelpiece.

Carly Beth followed her mother's gaze—and cried out in surprise. "It's—a head!"

"Not just *any* head," Mrs Caldwell said, beaming. "Go on. Take a closer look."

Carly Beth took a few steps towards the mantelpiece, her eyes on the head staring back at her. It took her a few moments to recognize the straight, brown hair, the brown eyes, the short snip of a nose, the round cheeks. "It's *me!*" she cried, walking up to it.

"Yes. Life size!" Mrs Caldwell declared. "I've just come from my art class at the museum. I finished it today. What do you think?"

Carly Beth picked it up and studied it closely. "It looks just like me, Mum. Really. What's it made of?"

"Plaster of Paris," her mother replied, taking it from Carly Beth and holding it up so that Carly Beth was face to face, eye to eye with herself. "You have to be careful. It's delicate. It's hollow, see?"

Carly Beth stared intently at the head, peering into her own eyes. "It—it's kind of creepy," she muttered.

"You mean because I did such a good job?" her mother demanded.

"It's just creepy, that's all," Carly Beth said. She forced herself to look away from the replica of herself, and saw that her mother's smile had faded.

Mrs Caldwell looked hurt. "Don't you like it?"

"Yeah. Of course. It's really good, Mum," Carly Beth answered quickly. "But, I mean, why on earth did you make it?"

"Because I love you," Mrs Caldwell replied curtly. "Why else? Honestly, Carly Beth, you have the strangest reactions to things. I worked really hard on this sculpture. I thought—"

"I'm sorry, Mum. I like it. Really, I do," Carly Beth insisted. "It was just a surprise, that's all. It's great. It looks just like me. I—I've had a bad day, that's all."

Carly Beth took another long look at the sculpture. Its brown eyes—*her* brown eyes—stared back at her. The brown hair shimmered in the afternoon sunlight through the window.

It smiled at me! Carly Beth thought, her mouth dropping open. I saw it! I just saw it smile!

No. It had to be a trick of the light.

It was a plaster of Paris head, she reminded herself.

Don't go scaring yourself over nothing, Carly Beth. Haven't you made a big enough fool of yourself today?

"Thanks for showing it to me, Mum," she said awkwardly, pulling her eyes away. She forced a smile. "Two heads are better than one, right?"

"Right," Mrs Caldwell agreed brightly. "Incidentally, Carly Beth, your duck costume is all ready. I put it on your bed."

"Huh? Duck costume?"

"You saw a duck costume at the shopping centre, remember?" Mrs Caldwell carefully placed the sculpted head on the mantelpiece. "The one with all the feathers and everything. You thought it would be funny to be a duck this Hallowe'en, so I made you a duck costume."

"Oh. Right," Carly Beth said, her mind spinning. Do I really want to be a stupid duck this Hallowe'en? she thought. "I'll go up and have a look at it, Mum. Thanks."

Carly Beth had forgotten all about the duck costume. I don't want to be cute this Hallowe'en, she thought as she climbed the stairs to her room. I want to be scary.

She had seen some really scary-looking masks in the window of a new party shop that had opened a few streets away from school. One of them, she knew, would be perfect.

But now she'd have to walk around in feathers and have everyone quack at her and make fun of her.

It wasn't fair. Why did her mother have to listen to every word she said?

Just because Carly Beth had admired a duck costume in a shop didn't mean she wanted to be a stupid duck for Hallowe'en!

Carly Beth hesitated outside her bedroom. The door had been pulled closed for some reason. She never closed the door.

She listened carefully. She thought she heard someone breathing on the other side of the door. Someone or some*thing*.

The breathing grew louder.

Carly Beth pressed an ear to the door.

What was in her room?

There was only one way to find out.

Carly Beth pulled open the door—and uttered a startled cry.

16

"*QUAAAAAAACCCK*!"

With a hideous cry, an enormous white-feathered duck, its eyes wild and frenzied, leapt at Carly Beth.

As she staggered backwards in astonishment, the duck knocked her over and pinned her to the hallway floor.

"QUAAACK! QUAAAACK!"

The costume has come alive!

That was Carly Beth's first frightened thought.

Then she quickly realized the truth. "Noah—get off me!" she demanded, trying to push the big duck off her chest.

The white feathers brushed against her nose. "Hey—that tickles!"

She sneezed.

"Noah—come *on*!"

"*QUAAAAAACK*!"

"Noah, I mean it!" she told her eight-year-old

brother. "What are you doing in my costume? It's supposed to be *my* costume."

"I was just trying it on," Noah said, his blue eyes staring down at her through the white-and-yellow duck mask. "Did I scare you?"

"Of course not," Carly Beth lied. "Now get up! You're heavy!"

He refused to budge.

"Why do you always want everything that's mine?" Carly Beth demanded angrily.

"I don't," he replied.

"And why do you think it's so funny to try and scare me all the time?" she asked.

"I can't help it if you get scared every time I say *boo*," he replied nastily.

"Get up! Get up!"

He quacked a few more times, flapping the feathery wings. Then he climbed to his feet. "Can I have this costume? It's really great."

Carly Beth frowned and shook her head. "You've got feathers all over me. You're moulting!"

"Moulting? What's *that* mean?" Noah demanded. He pulled off the mask. His blond hair was damp from sweat and matted against his head.

"It means you're going to be a bald duck!" Carly Beth told him.

"I don't care. Can I have this costume?" Noah asked, examining the mask. "It fits me. Really!"

18

"I don't know," Carly Beth told him. "Maybe." The phone rang in her room. "Get lost, okay? Go and fly south for the winter or something," she said, and hurried to answer the phone.

As she ran to her desk, she saw white feathers all over her bed. That costume will never survive till Hallowe'en! she thought.

She picked up the receiver. "Hello? Oh, hi, Sabrina. Yeah. I'm okay."

Sabrina had phoned to remind Carly Beth that the school Science Fair was tomorrow. They had to finish their project, a model of the solar system constructed with ping-pong balls.

"Come over after dinner," Carly Beth told her. "It's almost finished. We just have to paint it. My mum said she'd help us take it to school tomorrow."

They chatted for a while. Then Carly Beth confided, "I was so annoyed, Sabrina. At lunch today. Why do Chuck and Steve think it's so funny to do things like that to me?"

Sabrina was silent for a moment. "I think it's because you're so *scare-able*, Carly Beth."

"Scare-able?"

"You scream so easily," Sabrina said. "Other people get scared. But they're more quiet about it. You know Chuck and Steve. They don't really mean to be nasty. They just think it's funny."

"Well, I *don't* think it's funny at all," Carly

Beth replied unhappily. "And I'm not going to be *scare-able* any more. I mean it. I'm *not* ever going to scream or get frightened again."

The science projects were all set up for judging on the stage in the assembly hall. Mrs Armbruster, the head teacher, and Mr Smythe, the science teacher, walked from display to display, making notes on their clipboards.

The solar system, as designed by Carly Beth and Sabrina, had survived the trip to school in pretty good shape. Pluto had a slight dent in it, which the girls had struggled unsuccessfully to straighten out. And Earth kept coming loose from its string and bouncing across the floor. But both girls agreed the display looked pretty good.

Maybe it wasn't as impressive as Martin Goodman's project. Martin had built a computer from scratch. But Martin was a genius. And Carly Beth thought the judges didn't expect everyone else to be geniuses, too.

Looking around the crowded, noisy stage, Carly Beth saw other interesting projects. Mary Sue Chong had built some kind of electronic robot arm that could pick up a cup or wave to people. And Brian Baldwin had several glass bottles filled with brown gunky stuff that he claimed was toxic waste.

Someone had done a chemical analysis of the

town's drinking water. And someone had built a volcano that would erupt when the two judges came by.

"Our project is pretty boring," Sabrina whispered nervously to Carly Beth, her eyes on the two judges who were *oohing* and *aahing* over Martin Goodman's homemade computer. "I mean, it's just painted ping-pong balls on strings."

"I like our project," Carly Beth insisted. "We worked hard on it, Sabrina."

"I know," Sabrina replied fretfully. "But it's still pretty boring."

The volcano erupted, sending up a gush of red liquid. The judges appeared impressed. Several kids cheered.

"Uh-oh. Here they come," Carly Beth whispered, jamming her hands into her jeans pockets. Mrs Armbruster and Mr Smythe, smiles plastered across their faces, were coming closer.

They stopped to examine a display of light and crystals.

Suddenly, Carly Beth heard an excited shout from somewhere behind her on the stage. "My tarantula! Hey—my tarantula has escaped!"

She recognized Steve's voice.

"Where's my tarantula?" he called.

Several kids uttered startled cries. Some kids laughed.

21

I'm not going to get scared, Carly Beth told
herself, swallowing hard.

She knew she was terrified of tarantulas. But
this time she was determined not to show it.

"My tarantula—it got away!" Steve shouted
over the roar of excited voices.

I'm not going to get scared. I'm not going to get
scared, Carly Beth repeated to herself.

But then she felt something pinch the back of
her leg and dig its spiny pincer into her skin—
and Carly Beth uttered a shrill scream of terror
that rang out through the assembly hall.

Carly Beth screamed and knocked over the solar system.

She kicked her leg wildly, trying to shake off the tarantula. Ping-pong ball planets bounced over the floor.

She screamed again. "Get it off me! Get it *off*!"

"Carly Beth—stop!" Sabrina pleaded. "You're okay! You're okay!"

It took Carly Beth a long time to realize that everyone was laughing. Her heart pounding, she spun round to find Steve down on his hands and knees behind her.

He made a pinching motion with his thumb and finger. "Gotcha again," he said, grinning up at her.

"Noooo!" Carly Beth cried.

There was no tarantula, she realized. Steve had pinched her leg.

She raised her head and saw that kids all over the stage were laughing. Mrs Armbruster and

23

Mr Smythe were laughing, too.

With a cry of anger, Carly Beth tried to kick Steve in the side. But he spun away. She missed.

"Help me pick up the planets," she heard Sabrina say.

But Sabrina seemed far, far away.

All Carly Beth could hear was the pounding of her heart and the laughter of the kids all around her. Steve had climbed to his feet. He and Chuck were side by side, grinning at her, slapping each other high-fives.

"Carly Beth—help me," Sabrina pleaded.

But Carly Beth spun away, jumped off the stage, and ran, escaping up the gangway of the dark assembly hall.

I'm going to pay Steve and Chuck back, she vowed angrily, her trainers thudding loudly on the floor. I'm going to scare them, REALLY scare them!

But how?

24

"Okay. What time shall I meet you?" Carly Beth asked, cradling the phone between her chin and shoulder.

On the other end of the line, Sabrina considered for a moment. "How about seventhirty?"

It was Hallowe'en. The plan was to meet at Sabrina's house, then go trick-or-treating through the entire neighbourhood.

"The earlier the better. We'll get more chocolate," Sabrina said. "Did Steve phone you?"

"Yeah. He phoned," Carly Beth replied bitterly.

"Did he apologize?"

"Yeah, he apologized," Carly Beth muttered, rolling her eyes. "Big deal. I mean, he's already made me look like a jerk in front of the whole school. What good is an apology?"

"I think he felt guilty," Sabrina replied.

"I *hope* he felt guilty!" Carly Beth exclaimed. "It was so mean!"

"It was a dirty trick," Sabrina agreed. And then she added, "But you have to admit it was pretty funny."

"I don't have to admit anything!" Carly Beth snapped.

"Has it stopped raining?" Sabrina asked, changing the subject.

Carly Beth pulled back the curtain to glance out of her bedroom window. The evening sky was charcoal-grey. Dark clouds hovered low. But the rain had stopped. The street glistened wetly under the light of a streetlamp.

"No rain. I've got to go. See you at seven-thirty," Carly Beth said, speaking rapidly.

"Hey, wait. What's your costume?" Sabrina demanded.

"It's a surprise," Carly Beth told her, and hung up.

It'll be a surprise to me, too, she told herself, glancing unhappily at the feathery duck costume rolled up on the chair in the corner.

Carly Beth's plan had been to go to the new party shop after school and pick out the ugliest, most disgusting, scariest mask they had. But her mother had picked her up after school and insisted that she stay at home and watch Noah for a couple of hours.

Mrs Caldwell hadn't returned home until five-fifteen. Now it was nearly a quarter to six. There was no way the party shop would still be open, Carly Beth thought, frowning at the duck costume.

"Quack, quack," she said miserably.

She walked to the mirror and ran a hairbrush through her hair. Maybe it's worth a try, she thought. Maybe that shop stays open late on Hallowe'en.

She pulled open a drawer and took out her wallet. Did she have enough money for a good, scary mask?

Thirty dollars. Her life savings.

She folded the notes and stuffed them back into the wallet. Then, jamming the wallet into her jeans pocket, she grabbed her coat and hurried downstairs and out of the front door.

The evening air was cold and damp. Carly Beth struggled to zip up her coat as she jogged towards the party shop. The house next door had a glowing pumpkin lantern in the front window. The house on the corner had paper skeletons strung up across the front porch.

The wind howled through the bare trees. The branches above her head shook and rattled like bony arms.

What a creepy night, Carly Beth thought.

She started running a little faster. A car rolled

27

silently by, sending harsh white light floating across the pavement like a bright ghost.

Glancing across the street, Carly Beth saw the old Carpenter mansion looming over its dark, weed-choked lawn. Everyone said the ramshackle old house was haunted by people who had been murdered inside it a hundred years ago.

Once, Carly Beth had heard frightened howls coming from the old mansion. When she was Noah's age, Steve and Chuck and some other kids had dared each other to go up to the house and knock on the door. Carly Beth had run home instead. She never did find out if the other kids were brave enough to do it.

Now Carly Beth felt a chill of fear as she hurried past the old house. She knew this neighbourhood really well. She had lived in it all her life. But tonight it looked different to her.

Was it just the wet glow left by the rain?

No. It was a heavy feeling in the air. A heavier darkness. The eerie orange glow of grinning pumpkins in windows. The silent cries of ghouls and monsters waiting to float free on their night to celebrate. Hallowe'en.

Trying to force all the scary thoughts from her mind, Carly Beth turned the corner. The little party shop came into sight. The window was lit, revealing two rows of Hallowe'en masks, staring out at the street.

But was the shop still open?

Crossing her fingers, Carly Beth waited for a lorry to rumble past, then eagerly jogged across the street. She stopped for a second to examine the masks in the window. There were gorilla masks, monster masks, some sort of blue-haired alien mask.

Pretty good, she thought. These are pretty ugly. But they probably have even scarier ones inside.

The lights were on inside the shop. She peered through the glass door. Then she tried turning the knob.

It didn't move.

She tried again. She tried pulling the door open. Then she tried pushing.

No. No way.

She was too late. The shop was closed.

Carly Beth sighed and peered in through the glass. The walls of the tiny shop were covered with masks. The masks seemed to stare back at her.

They're laughing at me, she thought unhappily. Laughing at me because I'm too late. Because the shop is closed, and I'm going to have to be a stupid duck for Hallowe'en.

Suddenly, a dark shadow moved over the glass, blocking Carly Beth's view. She gasped and took a step back.

It took her a moment to realize that the shadow was a man. A man in a black suit, staring out at her, a look of surprise on his face.

"Are you—are you closed?" Carly Beth shouted through the glass.

The man gestured that he couldn't hear her. He turned the lock and pulled the door open a centimetre. "Can I help you?" he asked curtly.

He had shiny black hair, parted in the middle and slicked down on his head, and a pencil-thin black moustache.

"Are you open?" Carly Beth asked timidly. "I need a Hallowe'en mask."

"It's very late," the man replied, not answering her question. He pulled the door open another few centimetres. "We normally close at five."

"I really would like to buy a mask," Carly Beth told him in her most determined voice.

The man's tiny, black eyes peered into hers. His expression remained blank. "Come in," he said quietly.

As Carly Beth stepped past him into the shop, she saw that he wore a black cape. It must be a Hallowe'en costume, she told herself. I'm sure he doesn't wear that all the time.

She turned her attention to the masks on the two walls.

"What kind of mask are you looking for?" the man asked, closing the door behind him.

Carly Beth felt a stab of fear. His black eyes glowed like two burning coals. He seemed so strange. And here she was, locked in this closed shop with him.

"A s-scary one," she stammered.

He rubbed his chin thoughtfully. He pointed to the wall. "The gorilla mask has been very

31

popular. It has real hair. I believe I may have one left in stock."

Carly Beth stared up at the gorilla mask. She didn't really want to be a gorilla. It was too ordinary. It wasn't scary enough. "Hmmm . . . do you have anything scarier?" she asked.

He flipped his cape back over the shoulder of his black suit. "How about that yellowish one with the pointy ears?" he suggested, pointing. "I believe it's some sort of *Star Trek* character. I still have a few of them, I think."

"No." Carly Beth shook her head. "I need something really scary."

A strange smile formed under the man's thin moustache. His eyes burned into hers, as if trying to read her thoughts. "Look around," he said, with a sweep of his hand. "Everything I have left in stock is up on the walls."

Carly Beth turned her gaze to the masks. A pig mask with long, ugly tusks and blood trickling from the snout caught her eye. Pretty good, she thought. But not quite right.

A hairy werewolf mask with white, pointy fangs was hung beside it. Again, too ordinary, Carly Beth decided.

Her eyes glanced over a green Frankenstein mask, a Freddy Kreuger mask that came with Freddy's hand—complete with long, silvery blades for fingers—and an E.T. mask.

Just not scary enough, Carly Beth thought,

starting to feel a little desperate. *I need something that will really make Steve and Chuck die of fright!*

"Young lady, I am afraid I must ask you to make your choice," the man in the cape said softly. He had moved behind the narrow counter at the front and was turning a key in the cash register. "We are actually closed, after all."

"I'm sorry," Carly Beth started. "It's just that—"

The phone rang before she could finish explaining.

The man picked it up quickly and began talking in a low voice, turning his back to Carly Beth.

She wandered towards the back of the shop, studying the masks as she walked. She passed a black cat mask with long, ugly yellow fangs. A vampire mask with bright red blood trickling down its lips was hung next to a grinning, bald mask of Uncle Fester from *The Addams Family*.

Not right, not right, not right, Carly Beth thought, frowning.

She hesitated when she spotted a narrow door slightly ajar at the back of the shop. Was there another room? Were there more masks back there?

She glanced to the front. The man, hidden

behind his cape, still had his back to her as he talked on the phone.

Carly Beth gave the door a hesitant push to peep inside. The door creaked open. Pale orange light washed over the small, shadowy back room.

Carly Beth stepped inside—and gasped in amazement.

Two dozen empty eye sockets stared blindly at Carly Beth.

She gaped in horror at the distorted, deformed faces.

They were masks, she realized. Two shelves of masks. But the masks were so ugly, so grotesque—so *real*—they made her breath catch in her throat.

Carly Beth gripped the doorframe, reluctant to enter the tiny back room. Staring into the dim orange light, she studied the hideous masks.

One mask had long, stringy yellow hair falling over its bulging, green forehead. A hairy black rat's head poked up from a knot in the hair, the rat's eyes gleaming like two dark jewels.

The mask beside it had a large nail stuck through an eyehole. Thick, wet-looking blood poured from the eye, down the cheek.

Chunks of rotting skin appeared to be falling

35

off another mask, revealing grey bone underneath. An enormous black insect, some kind of grotesque beetle, poked out from between the green-and-yellow decayed teeth.

Carly Beth's horror mixed with excitement. She took a step into the room. The wooden floorboards creaked noisily beneath her.

She took another step closer to the grotesque, grinning masks. They seemed so real, so horribly real. The faces had such detail. The skin appeared to be made of flesh, not rubber or plastic.

These are perfect! she thought, her heart pounding. These are just what I was looking for. They look *terrifying* just propped up on these shelves!

She imagined Steve and Chuck seeing one of these masks coming at them in the dark of night. She pictured herself uttering a bloodcurdling scream and leaping out from behind a tree in one of them.

She imagined the horrified expressions on the boys' faces. She pictured Steve and Chuck shrieking in terror and running for their lives.

Perfect. Perfect!

What a laugh that would be. What a victory!

Carly Beth took a deep breath and stepped up to the shelves. Her eyes settled on an ugly mask on the lower shelf.

It had a bulging, bald head. Its skin was a

putrid yellow-green. Its enormous, sunken eyes were an eerie orange and seemed to glow. It had a broad, flat nose, smashed in like a skeleton's nose. The dark-lipped mouth gaped wide, revealing jagged animal fangs.

Staring hard at the hideous mask, Carly Beth reached out a hand towards it. Reluctantly, she touched the broad forehead.

And as she touched it, the mask cried out.

"Ohh!"

Carly Beth shrieked and jerked back her hand.

The mask grinned at her. Its orange eyes glowed brightly. The lips appeared to curl back over the fangs.

She suddenly felt dizzy. *What is going on here?*

As she staggered back, away from the shelves, she realized that the angry cry hadn't come from the mask.

It had come from behind her.

Carly Beth spun round to see the black-caped shop owner glaring at her from the doorway. His dark eyes flashed. His mouth was turned down into a menacing frown.

"Oh. I thought—" Carly Beth started, glancing back at the mask. She still felt confused. Her heart pounded loudly in her chest.

"I am sorry you saw these," the man said in a

low, threatening voice. He took a step towards her, his cape brushing the doorway.

What is he going to do? Carly Beth wondered, uttering a horrified gasp. Why is he coming at me like that?

What is he going to do to me?

"I am so sorry," he repeated, his small, dark eyes burning into hers. He took another step closer.

Carly Beth backed away from him. Then she uttered a startled cry as she backed into the display shelves.

The hideous masks jiggled and quaked, as if alive.

"What—what do you mean?" she managed to choke out. "I—I was just—"

"I am sorry you saw these because they are not for sale," the man said softly.

He stepped past her and straightened one of the masks on its stand.

Carly Beth breathed a loud sigh of relief. He didn't mean to scare me, she told herself. I am scaring myself.

She crossed her arms in front of her coat and tried to force her heartbeat to return to normal. She stepped to the side as the shop owner continued to arrange the masks, handling them carefully, brushing their hair with one hand, tenderly dusting off their bulging, blood-covered foreheads.

"Not for sale? Why not?" Carly Beth demanded. Her voice came out tiny and shrill.

"Too scary," the man replied. He turned to smile at her.

"But I want a really scary one," Carly Beth told him. "I want *that* one." She pointed to the mask she had touched, the mask with the open mouth and the terrifying, jagged fangs.

"Too scary," the man repeated, pushing his cape behind his shoulder.

"But it's Hallowe'en!" Carly Beth protested.

"I have a really scary gorilla mask," the man said, motioning for Carly Beth to go back to the front room. "Very scary. Looks like it's growling. I will give you a good price on it since it's so late."

Carly Beth shook her head, her arms crossed defiantly in front of her. "A gorilla mask won't scare Steve and Chuck," she said.

The man's expression changed. "Who?"

"My friends," she told him. "I *have* to have that one," she insisted. "It's so scary, I'm almost afraid to touch it. It's perfect."

"It's too scary," the man repeated, lowering his eyes to it. He ran his hand over the green forehead. "I can't take the responsibility."

"It's so real looking!" Carly Beth gushed. "They'll both faint. I know they will. Then they'll never try to scare me again."

"Young lady—" the shop owner started,

40

glancing impatiently at his watch. "I really must insist that you make up your mind. I am a patient man, but—"

"Please!" Carly Beth begged. "Please sell it to me! Here. Look." She dug into her jeans pocket and pulled out the money she had brought.

"Young lady, I—"

"Thirty dollars," Carly Beth said, shoving the folded-up notes into the man's hand. "I'll give you thirty dollars for it. That's enough, isn't it?"

"It's not a matter of money," he told her. "These masks are not for sale." With an exasperated sigh, he started towards the doorway that led to the front of the shop.

"Please! I *need* it. I really *need* it!" Carly Beth begged, chasing after him.

"These masks are too real," he insisted, gesturing to the shelves. "I'm warning you—"

"Please? Please?"

He shut his eyes. "You will be sorry."

"No, I won't. I won't. I *know* I won't!" Carly Beth exclaimed gleefully, seeing that he was about to give in.

He opened his eyes. He shook his head. She could see that he was debating with himself.

With a sigh, he tucked the money into his coat pocket. Then he carefully lifted the mask from the shelf, straightening the pointed ears, and started to hand it to her.

"Thanks!" she cried, eagerly snatching the mask from his hands. "It's perfect! Perfect!"

She held the mask by the flat nose. It felt soft and surprisingly warm. "Thanks again!" she cried, hurrying to the front, the mask gripped tightly in her hand.

"Can I give you a bag for it?" the man called after her.

But Carly Beth was already out of the shop.

She crossed the street and started to run towards home. The sky was black. No stars poked through. The street still glistened wetly from the afternoon's rain.

This is going to be the best trick-or-treat night ever, Carly Beth thought happily. Because this is the night I get my revenge.

She couldn't wait to spring out at Steve and Chuck. She wondered what their costumes would be. They had both talked about painting their faces and dyeing their hair blue and being Smurfs.

Pathetic. Really lame.

Carly Beth stopped under a streetlight and held up the mask, gripping it with both hands by its pointed ears. It grinned up at her, the two crooked rows of fangs hanging over its thick, rubbery lips.

Then, tucking it carefully under one arm, she ran the rest of the way home.

Stopping at the bottom of the drive, she gazed

up at her house, the front windows all glowing brightly, the porchlight sending white light over the lawn.

I've *got* to try this mask out on someone, she thought eagerly. I've *got* to see just how good it is.

Her brother's grinning face popped into her mind.

"Noah. Of course," she said aloud. "Noah has really been asking for it."

Grinning gleefully, Carly Beth hurried up the drive, eager to make Noah her first victim.

Carly Beth crept silently through the front door and tossed her coat onto the hall floor. The house felt stuffy and hot. A sweet smell, the aroma of hot cider on the stove, greeted her.

Mum really gets into holidays, she thought with a smile.

Tiptoeing through the front hallway, holding the mask in front of her, Carly Beth listened hard.

Noah, where are you?

Where are you, my little guinea pig?

Noah was always bragging about how he was so much braver than Carly Beth. He was always putting insects down her back and planting rubber snakes in her bed—anything he could think of to make her scream.

She heard footsteps above her head. Noah must be up in his room, she realized. He's probably putting on his Hallowe'en costume.

At the last minute, Noah had decided he

wanted to be a cockroach. Mrs Caldwell had dashed frantically all over the house, finding the materials to build pointy feelers and a hard shell for his back.

Well, the little creep is in for a surprise, Carly Beth thought evilly. She examined her mask. This should send that cockroach scampering under the sink!

She stopped at the bottom of the stairs. She could hear loud music coming from Noah's room. An old heavy-metal song.

Gripping the mask by the rubbery neck, she raised it carefully over her head, then pulled it slowly down.

It was surprisingly warm inside. The mask fitted tighter than Carly Beth had imagined. It had a funny smell, kind of sour, kind of old, like damp newspapers that have been left for years in an attic or garage.

She slid it all the way down until she could see through the eyeholes. Then she smoothed the bulging, bald head over her head and tugged the neck down.

I should have stopped in front of a mirror, she fretted. I can't see if it looks right.

The mask felt very tight. Her breathing echoed noisily in the flat nose. She forced herself to ignore the sour smell that invaded her nose.

She held on tightly to the banister as she crept

45

up the stairs. It was hard to see the steps through the eyeholes. She had to take the climb slowly, one step at a time.

The heavy-metal music ended as she stepped onto the landing. She crept silently down the hall and stopped outside Noah's door.

Carly Beth edged her head into the doorway and peeked into the brightly lit room. Noah was standing in front of the mirror, adjusting the two long cockroach feelers above his head.

"Noah—I'm coming for you!" Carly Beth called.

To her surprise, her voice came out gruff and low. It wasn't her voice at all!

"Huh?" Startled, Noah spun round.

"Noah—I've *got* you!" Carly Beth shrieked, her voice deep, raspy, evil.

"No!" her brother uttered a hushed cry of protest. Even under his insect make-up, Carly Beth could see him go pale.

She darted into the room, her arms outstretched as if ready to grab him.

"No—*please!*" he cried, his expression terrified. "Who *are* you? How—how did you get in?"

He doesn't even recognize me! Carly Beth thought gleefully.

And he's scared to death!

Was it the hideous face? The deep rumble of a voice? Or both?

Carly Beth didn't care. The mask was *definitely* a success!

"I've *GOT* you!" she screamed, surprising herself at how scary her voice sounded from inside the mask.

"No! Please!" Noah begged. "Mum! *Mum!*" He backed towards the bed, trembling all over, his feelers quivering in fright. "Mum! *Hellllp!*"

Carly Beth burst out laughing. The laughter came out in a deep rumble. "It's me, stupid!" she cried. "What a yellow-bellied scaredy-cat!"

"Huh?" Still huddled by the bed, Noah stared hard at her.

"Don't you recognize my jeans? My sweater? It's me, you idiot!" Carly Beth declared in the gruff voice.

"But your face—that mask!" Noah stammered. "It—it really scared me. I mean—" He gaped at her, studying the mask. "It didn't sound like you, Carly Beth," he muttered. "I thought—"

Carly Beth tugged at the bottom of the mask, trying to lift it off. It felt hot and sticky. She was panting noisily.

She tried pulling the bottom with both hands. The mask didn't budge.

She raised her hands to the pointed ears and

tried lifting it off. She tugged. Tugged harder.

She tried pulling the mask off by the top of the head. It didn't move.

"Hey—it won't come off!" she cried. "The mask—it won't come off!"

"What's going on here?" Carly Beth cried, tugging at the mask with both hands.

"Stop it!" Noah cried. His voice sounded angry, but his eyes revealed fear. "Stop kidding around, Carly Beth. You're scaring me!"

"I'm *not* kidding around," Carly Beth insisted in her harsh, raspy voice. "I really can't—get—this—off!"

"Take it off! You're not funny!" her brother shouted.

With great effort, Carly Beth managed to slip her fingers under the neck of the mask. Then, she pulled it away from her skin and lifted it off her head.

"Whew!"

The air felt so cool and sweet. She shook her hair free. Then she playfully tossed the mask at Noah. "Good mask, huh?" She grinned at him.

He let the mask bounce onto the bed. Then he picked it up hesitantly and examined it.

"Where'd you get it?" he asked, poking a finger against the ugly fangs.

"At that new party shop," she told him, wiping perspiration from her forehead. "It's so hot inside it."

"Can I try it on?" Noah asked, pushing his fingers through the eyeholes.

"Not now. I'm late," she replied sharply. She laughed. "You certainly looked scared."

He tossed the mask back at her, frowning. "I was just pretending," he said. "I knew it was you."

"Yeah, sure!" she replied, rolling her eyes. "That's why you screamed like a maniac."

"I did *not* scream," Noah protested. "I was just putting on an act. For you."

"Yeah. Right," Carly Beth muttered. She turned and headed towards the door, rolling the mask over her hand.

"How'd you change your voice like that?" Noah called after her.

Carly Beth stopped at the doorway and turned back to him. Her smile gave way to a puzzled expression.

"That deep voice was the scariest part," Noah said, staring at the mask in her hand. "How did you do that?"

"I don't know," Carly Beth replied thoughtfully. "I really don't know."

By the time she got to her room, she was grinning again. The mask had worked. It had been a wonderful success.

Noah might not want to admit it, but when Carly Beth had burst in on him, growling through the hideous mask, he'd nearly jumped out of his cockroach shell.

Look out, Chuck and Steve! she thought gleefully. You're next!

She sat down on her bed and glanced at the clock radio on her bedside table. She had a few minutes until it was time to meet everyone in front of Sabrina's house.

Time enough to think of the best possible way to give them the scare of their lives.

I don't want to just jump out at them, Carly Beth thought, playing her fingers over the sharp fangs. That's too boring.

I want to do something they'll remember.

Something they'll never forget.

She ran her hands over the mask's pointy ears. Suddenly she had an idea.

Carly Beth pulled the old broom handle from the cupboard. She brushed off a thick ball of dust and examined the long, wooden pole.

Perfect, she thought.

She checked to make sure her mother was still in the kitchen. Carly Beth was sure her mother wouldn't approve of what she was about to do. Mrs Caldwell still thought that Carly Beth was going to wear the duck costume.

Tiptoeing silently into the living room, Carly Beth stepped up to the mantelpiece and pulled down the plaster of Paris head her mother had sculpted.

It really does look just like me, Carly Beth thought, holding the sculpture waist high and studying it carefully. It's so lifelike. Mum is really talented.

Carefully, she placed the head on the broomstick. It balanced easily.

She carried it over to the hallway mirror. It

looks as if I'm carrying my real head on a stick, Carly Beth thought, admiring it. A wide grin broke out across her face. Her eyes sparkled gleefully.

Excellent!

She leaned the head and stick against the wall and pulled on the mask. Once again, the sour aroma rushed into her nostrils. The heat of the mask seemed to wrap around her.

The mask tightened against her skin as she pulled it down.

Raising her eyes to the mirror, she nearly frightened *herself!* It's like a real face, she thought, unable to take her eyes away. My eyes seem a part of it. It doesn't look as if I'm peering out of eyeholes.

She moved the gruesome mouth up and down a few times. It moves like a real mouth, she realized.

It doesn't look like a mask at all.

It looks like a gross, deformed face.

Working with both hands, she flattened the bulging forehead, smoothing it over her hair.

Excellent! she repeated to herself, feeling her excitement grow. *Excellent!*

The mask is perfect! she decided. She couldn't believe the man in the party shop didn't want to sell it to her. It was the scariest, realest, ugliest mask she had ever seen.

I will be the terror of Maple Avenue tonight!

53

Carly Beth decided, admiring herself in the mirror. Kids will be having nightmares about me for weeks!

Especially Chuck and Steve, she told herself.

"Boo!" she muttered to herself, pleased to hear that the gruff voice had returned. "I'm ready."

She picked up the broomstick, carefully balanced her sculpted head on top of it, and started for the door.

Her mother's voice stopped her. "Carly Beth—wait a minute," Mrs Caldwell called from the kitchen. "I want to see how you look in that duck costume!"

"Uh-oh," Carly Beth groaned out loud. "Mum isn't going to like this."

54

Carly Beth froze in the doorway. She could hear her mother's footsteps approaching in the hallway.

"Let me see you, dear," Mrs Caldwell called. "Did the costume fit?"

Maybe I should've told her about my change of plans, Carly Beth thought guiltily. I would've said something, but I didn't want to hurt Mum's feelings.

Now she's in for a shock. And she's going to be really angry when she sees I've borrowed her sculpture.

She's going to make me put it back on the mantelpiece.

She's going to ruin everything.

"I'm in a bit of a hurry, Mum," Carly Beth called, her voice deep and raspy inside the mask. "I'll see you later, okay?" She pulled open the front door.

"You can wait one second while I see my

costume on you," her mother called. She rounded the corner and came into view.

I'm sunk, Carly Beth thought with a groan.

I'm caught.

The phone rang. The sound echoed loudly inside Carly Beth's mask.

Her mother stopped and turned back to the kitchen. "Oh, drat. I'd better answer that. It's probably your father phoning from Chicago." She disappeared back to the kitchen. "I'll have to see you later, Carly Beth. Be careful, okay?"

Carly Beth breathed a sigh of relief. Saved by the bell, she thought.

Balancing the head on the broomstick, she hurried out of the door. She closed the door behind her and jogged down the front path.

It had become a clear, cool night. A pale halfmoon rose low over the bare trees. Fat brown leaves swirled around her ankles as she headed for the pavement.

The plan was to meet Chuck and Steve in front of Sabrina's house. Carly Beth couldn't wait.

Her head bobbed and bounced on the broomstick as she ran. The house on the corner had been decorated for Hallowe'en. Orange lights ran along the top of the porch. Two large, smiling cut out pumpkins stood beside the doorway. A cardboard skeleton had been propped up

56

at the end of the front path.

I *love* Hallowe'en! Carly Beth thought happily. She crossed the street onto Sabrina's road.

On other Hallowe'en nights, she had been frightened. Her friends were always playing mean tricks on her. Last year, Steve had slipped a very real-looking rubber rat into her trick-or-treat bag.

When Carly Beth had reached into the bag, she'd felt something soft and hairy. She'd pulled out the rat and shrieked at the top of her voice. She was so scared, she'd spilled her sweets all over the drive.

Chuck and Steve thought it was a riot. So did Sabrina. They always spoiled Hallowe'en for her. They thought it was so hilarious to scare Carly Beth and make her scream.

Well, this year I won't be the one screaming, she thought. This year, I'll be the one making everyone else scream.

Sabrina's house was at the end of the road. As Carly Beth hurried towards it, bare tree limbs shivered above her. The halfmoon disappeared behind a heavy cloud, and the ground darkened.

The head on the broom handle bounced and nearly fell off. Carly Beth slowed her pace. She glanced up at the head, shifting her grip on the broomstick.

The eyes on the sculpted head stared straight

ahead, as if searching out trouble. In the darkness, the head looked real. The shadows moving over it as Carly Beth walked under the bare tree limbs made the eyes and mouth appear to move.

Hearing laughter, Carly Beth turned. Across the street, a group of trick-or-treaters was invading a brightly lit front porch. In the yellow porchlight, Carly Beth saw a ghost, a Mutant Hero Turtle, a Freddy Kreuger, and a princess in a pink ballgown and a tinfoil crown. The kids were little. Two mothers watched them from the foot of the drive.

Carly Beth watched them get their sweets. Then she walked the rest of the way to Sabrina's house. She climbed the front step, stepping into a white triangle of light from the porchlight. She could hear voices inside the house, Sabrina shouting something to her mother, a TV on in the living room.

Carly Beth adjusted her mask with her free hand. She straightened the gaping, fanged mouth. Then she checked to make sure the head was balanced on the broomstick.

She reached to ring Sabrina's doorbell—then stopped.

Voices behind her.

She turned and squinted into the darkness. Two costumed boys were approaching, shoving each other playfully on the pavement.

Chuck and Steve!

I'm just in time, Carly Beth thought happily. She leapt off the step and crouched behind a low evergreen bush.

Okay, boys, she thought eagerly, her heart pounding. Get ready for a scare.

Carly Beth peered over the top of the bush. The two boys were halfway up the drive.

It was too dark to get a good look at their costumes. One of them wore a long overcoat and a wide-brimmed, Indiana Jones fedora. She couldn't really see the other one.

Carly Beth took a deep breath and prepared to leap out at them. She gripped the broomstick tightly.

My whole body is trembling, she realized. The mask suddenly felt hot, as if her excitement had heated it up. Her breath rattled noisily in the flat nose.

Walking slowly, playfully shoving each other with their shoulders like football players, the boys made their way up the drive. One of them said something Carly Beth couldn't hear. The other one laughed loudly, a high-pitched giggle.

Peering into the darkness, Carly Beth

60

watched them until they were nearly right in front of the bush.

Okay—now! she declared silently.

Raising the broomstick with its staring head on the top, she leapt out.

The boys shrieked, startled.

She could see their dark eyes go wide as they gaped at her mask.

A ferocious roar escaped her throat. A deep, rumbling howl that frightened even her.

At the terrifying sound, both boys cried out again. One of them actually dropped to his knees on the drive.

They both stared up at the head, bobbing on the broomstick. It seemed to glare down at them.

Another howl escaped Carly Beth's throat. It started low, as if coming from far away, and then pierced the air, raspy and deep, like the roar of an angry creature.

"Noooo!" one of the boys cried.

"Who *are* you?" the other cried. "Leave us alone!"

Carly Beth heard rapid footsteps crunching over the dead leaves on the drive. Looking up, she saw a woman in a bulky coat running up the drive.

"Hey—what are you doing?" the woman demanded, her voice shrill and angry. "Are you scaring my kids?"

"Huh?" Carly Beth swallowed hard. She turned her eyes back to the two frightened boys.

"Wait!" she cried, realizing they weren't Chuck and Steve.

"What are you doing?" the woman repeated breathlessly. She stepped up to the two boys and put a hand on each of their shoulders. "Are you two okay?"

"Yeah. We're okay, Mum," the one in the overcoat and fedora replied.

The other boy wore white make-up and a red clown nose. "She—she jumped out at us," he told his mother, avoiding Carly Beth's stare. "She kind of scared us."

The woman turned angrily to Carly Beth and shook her finger at her accusingly. "Don't you have anything better to do than to scare two young boys? Why don't you pick on someone your own age?"

Normally Carly Beth would have apologized. She would have explained to the woman that she'd made a mistake, that she meant to scare two different boys.

But hidden behind the ugly mask, still hearing the strange howl that had burst so unexpectedly from her throat, she didn't feel like apologizing.

She felt . . . anger. And she wasn't sure why.

"*Go away!*" she rasped, waving the broomstick

menacingly. The head—*her* head—stared down at the two startled boys.

"*What* did you say?" their mother demanded, her voice tight with growing outrage. "*What* did you say?"

"I said *go away!*" Carly Beth snarled in a voice so deep, so terrifying, that it frightened even her.

The woman crossed her arms in front of the heavy, down coat. Her eyes narrowed on Carly Beth. "Who are you? What is your name?" she demanded. "Do you live around here?"

"Mum—let's just go," the boy with the clown face urged, tugging at her coat sleeve.

"Yeah. Come on," his brother pleaded.

"*Go away. I'm WARNING you!*" Carly Beth growled.

The woman stood her ground, her arms tightly crossed, her eyes narrowed at Carly Beth. "Just because it's Hallowe'en doesn't give you the right—"

"Mum, we want to get some sweets!" the clown pleaded, tugging his mother's sleeve harder. "Come on!"

"We're wasting the whole night!" his brother complained.

Carly Beth was breathing hard, her breath escaping the mask in low, noisy grunts. I sound like an animal, she thought, puzzled. What is happening to me?

She could feel her anger growing. Her breathing rattled noisily in the tight mask. Her face felt burning hot.

Her anger raged through her chest. Her whole body was trembling. She felt about to burst.

I'm going to tear this woman apart! Carly Beth decided.

I'll chew her to bits! I'll tear her skin off her bones! Furious thoughts raged through Carly Beth's mind.

She tensed her muscles, crouched low, and prepared to pounce.

But before she could make her move, the two boys pulled their mother away.

"Let's go, Mum."

"Yeah. Let's go. She's *crazy*!"

Yeah. I'm crazy. Crazy, crazy, CRAZY. The word repeated, roaring through Carly Beth's mind. The mask grew hotter, tighter.

The woman gave Carly Beth one last cold stare. Then she turned and led the two boys down the drive.

Carly Beth stared after them, panting loudly. She had a strong urge to chase after them—to *really* scare them!

But a loud cry made her stop and spin round.

Sabrina stood on the front step, leaning on the

screen door, her mouth open in a wide O of surprise. "Who's there?" she cried, squinting into the darkness.

Sabrina was dressed as Cat Woman, with a silver-and-grey catsuit beneath a silver mask. Her black hair was pulled tightly behind her head. Her dark eyes stared intently at Carly Beth.

"Don't you recognize me?" Carly Beth rasped, stepping closer.

She could see the fright in Sabrina's eyes. Sabrina gripped the door handle tightly, standing half in and half out of her house.

"Don't you recognize me, Sabrina?" She waved the head on the broomstick, as if giving her friend a clue.

Sabrina gasped and raised her hand to her mouth as she noticed the head on the pole. "Carly Beth—is that—is that *you*?" she stammered. Her eyes darted from the mask to the head, then back again.

"Hi, Sabrina," Carly Beth growled. "It's me."

Sabrina continued to study her. "That mask!" she cried finally. "It's *excellent*! Really. Excellent. It's so scary."

"I like your catsuit," Carly Beth told her, stepping closer, into the light.

Sabrina's eyes were raised to the top of the broomstick. "That head—it's so real! Where did you get it?"

"It's my *real* head!" Carly Beth joked.

Sabrina continued to stare at it. "Carly Beth, when I first saw it, I—"

"My mum made it," Carly Beth told her. "In her art class."

"I thought it was a real head," Sabrina said. She shivered. "The eyes. The way they stare at you."

Carly Beth shook the broomstick, making the head nod.

Sabrina studied Carly Beth's mask. "Wait till Chuck and Steve see your costume."

I can't wait! Carly Beth thought darkly. "Where are they?" she demanded, glancing back to the street.

"Steve called," Sabrina replied. "He said they'd be late. He has to take his little sister trick-or-treating before he can meet us."

Carly Beth sighed, disappointed.

"We'll start without them," Sabrina suggested. "They can catch up with us later."

"Yeah. Okay," Carly Beth replied.

"I'll get my coat and we can go," Sabrina said. She took one last, lingering look at the head on the broomstick, then the storm door slammed shut with a *bang* as she disappeared inside to get her coat.

The wind picked up as the two girls made their way down the road. Dead leaves swirled at their feet. The bare trees bent and shivered. Above the dark, sloping roofs, the pale half-moon slipped in and out of the clouds.

Sabrina chattered about all the problems she'd had with her costume. The first catsuit she'd bought had a long run in one leg and had to be returned. Then Sabrina couldn't find a cat-eyed mask that looked right.

Carly Beth remained quiet. She couldn't hide her disappointment that Chuck and Steve hadn't met them as planned.

What if they never catch up with us? she wondered. What if we don't see them at all?

The whole point of the night, as far as Carly Beth was concerned, was meeting the two boys and scaring the living daylights out of them.

Sabrina had given her a shopping bag to put her sweets in. As they walked, Carly Beth gripped the bag in one hand, struggling to keep the head balanced on the pole in her other hand.

"So where did you buy your mask? Your mother didn't *make* it, did she? Did you go to that new party shop? Can I touch it?"

Sabrina always talked a lot. But tonight she was going for the world record for nonstop chatter.

Carly Beth obediently stopped so that her friend could touch the mask. Sabrina pressed her fingers against the cheek, then instantly jerked them back.

68

"Oh! It feels like skin!"

Carly Beth laughed, a scornful laugh she had never heard before.

"Yuck! What's it made of?" Sabrina demanded. "It isn't skin—*is* it? It's some kind of rubber, right?"

"I suppose so," Carly Beth muttered.

"Then how come it's so warm?" Sabrina asked. "Is it uncomfortable to wear? You must be sweating like a pig."

Feeling a surge of rage, Carly Beth dropped the bag and the broomstick.

"Shut up! Shut up! Shut up!" she snarled.

Then with an angry howl, she grabbed Sabrina's throat with both hands and began to choke her.

Sabrina uttered a shocked cry and staggered back, pulling herself from Carly Beth's grip. "C-Carly Beth!" she spluttered.

What is happening to me? Carly Beth wondered, gaping in horror at her friend. Why did I do that?

"Uh . . . gotcha!" Carly Beth exclaimed. She laughed. "You should have seen the look on your face, Sabrina. Did you think I was really choking you?"

Sabrina rubbed her neck with one silver-gloved hand. She frowned at her friend. "That was a joke? You scared me to death!"

Carly Beth laughed again. "Just keeping in character," she said lightly, pointing to her mask. "You know. Trying to get in the right mood. Ha-ha. I *like* scaring people. Usually I'm the one who's trembling in fright."

She picked up the bag and broomstick, fixing the plaster of Paris head on the top. Then she hurried up the nearest drive towards a well-lit house with a HAPPY HALLOWE'EN banner in the front window.

Does Sabrina believe it was just a joke? Carly Beth asked herself as she raised her shopping bag and rang the doorbell. What on earth was I doing?

Why did I suddenly get so angry? Why did I attack my best friend like that?

Sabrina stepped up beside her as the front door was pulled open. Two little blonde kids, a boy and a girl, appeared in the doorway. Their mother came up behind them.

"Trick or Treat!" Carly Beth and Sabrina called out in unison.

"Ooh, that's a scary mask!" the woman said to her two children, grinning at Carly Beth.

"What are you supposed to be? A cat?" the little boy asked Sabrina.

Sabrina meowed at him. "I'm Cat Woman," she told him.

"I don't like the other one!" the little girl exclaimed to her mother. "It's too scary."

"It's just a funny mask," the mother assured her daughter.

"Too scary. It's *scaring* me!" the little girl insisted.

Carly Beth leaned into the doorway of the house, bringing her grotesque face up close to the little girl. *"I'll eat you up!"* she growled nastily.

The little girl screamed and disappeared into the house. Her brother stared wide-eyed at Carly Beth. The mother quickly dropped chocolate bars into the girls' bags. "You shouldn't have scared her," she said softly. "She has nightmares."

Instead of apologizing, Carly Beth turned to the little boy. *"I'll eat you up too!"* she snarled.

"Hey—stop!" the woman protested.

Carly Beth laughed a deep-throated laugh, jumped off the porch, and took off across the front lawn.

"Why'd you do that?" Sabrina asked as they made their way across the street. "Why'd you scare those kids like that?"

"The mask made me do it," Carly Beth replied. She meant it as a joke. But the thought troubled her mind.

At the next few houses, Carly Beth hung back and let Sabrina do the talking. At one house, a middle-aged man in a torn blue sweater pretended to be scared of Carly Beth's mask. His wife insisted that the girls come inside so that they could show their elderly mother the great costumes.

Carly Beth groaned loudly, but followed Sabrina into the house. The old woman gazed at them blankly from her wheelchair. Carly Beth growled at her, but it didn't appear to make any impression.

On their way out of the door, the man in the torn sweater handed each girl a green apple. Carly Beth waited till they were down on the pavement. Then she turned, pulled back her arm, and heaved the apple at the man's house with all her might.

It made a loud *thunk* as it smacked against the shingled front wall near the front door.

"I really *hate* getting apples on Hallowe'en!" Carly Beth declared. "Especially green ones!"

"Carly Beth—I'm worried about you!" Sabrina cried, eyeing her friend with concern. "You're not acting like you at all."

No. I'm not a pitiful, frightened little mouse tonight, Carly Beth thought bitterly.

"Give me that," she ordered Sabrina, and grabbed Sabrina's apple from her bag.

"Hey—stop!" Sabrina protested.

But Carly Beth arched her arm and tossed Sabrina's apple at the house. It clanged noisily as it hit the aluminium gutter.

The man in the torn sweater poked his head out of the door. "Hey—what's the big idea?"

"Run!" Carly Beth screamed.

The two girls took off, running at full speed down the street. They didn't stop until the house was out of sight.

Sabrina grabbed Carly Beth's shoulders and held on, struggling to catch her breath. "You're crazy!" she gasped. "You're really crazy!"

"It takes one to know one," Carly Beth said playfully.

They both laughed.

Carly Beth searched the street, looking for Chuck and Steve. She saw a small group of costumed kids huddled together on the corner. But no sign of the two boys.

Smaller houses, jammed closer together, lined the two sides of this block. "Let's split up," Carly Beth suggested, leaning against the broomstick. "We'll get more sweets that way."

Sabrina frowned at her friend, eyeing her suspiciously. "Carly Beth, you don't even *like* sweets!" she exclaimed.

But Carly Beth was already running up the drive to the first house, her sculpted head bobbing wildly above her on its broomstick.

This is my night, Carly Beth thought, accepting a chocolate bar from the smiling woman who answered the door. *My night!*

She felt a tingle of excitement she'd never felt before. And a strange feeling she couldn't describe. A hunger . . .

A few minutes later, her shopping bag starting to feel heavy, she came to the end of the street. She hesitated on the corner, trying to

74

decide whether to do the other side of the street or go on to the next block.

It was very dark there, she realized. The moon had once again disappeared behind dark clouds. The corner streetlight was out, probably burned out.

Across the street, four very young trick or treaters were giggling as they approached a house with a pumpkin-lantern on the porch.

Carly Beth sank back into the darkness. She heard voices, boys' voices.

Chuck and Steve?

No. The voices were unfamiliar. They were arguing about where to trick-or-treat next. One of them wanted to go home and phone a friend.

How about a little scare for you boys? Carly Beth thought, a smile spreading across her face. *How about something to remember this Hallowe'en night?*

She waited, listening, until they were a few metres away. She could see them now. Two mummies, their faces wrapped in gauze.

Closer, closer. She waited for the perfect moment.

Then she burst from the shadows, uttering an angry animal howl that shattered the air.

The two boys gasped and jumped back.

"Hey—!" One of them tried to shout, but his voice caught in his throat.

The other one dropped his bag of sweets.

As he started to pick it up, Carly Beth moved quickly. She grabbed the bag from his hand, jerked it away from him, and started to run.

"Come back!"

"That's *mine*!"

"Hey—"

Their voices were high and shrill, filled with fear and surprise. As she ran across the street, Carly Beth glanced back to see if they were following her.

No. They were too frightened. They stood huddled together on the corner, shouting after her.

Holding the stolen bag tightly in her free hand, Carly Beth tossed back her head and laughed. A cruel laugh, a triumphant laugh. A laugh she had never heard before.

She emptied the boy's sweets into her own bag, then tossed his bag onto the ground.

She felt good, really good. Really strong. And ready for more fun.

Come on, Chuck and Steve, she thought. *It's YOUR turn next!*

Carly Beth found Chuck and Steve a few minutes later.

They were across the street from her, standing in the light of someone's driveway, examining the contents of their trick-or-treat bags.

Carly Beth ducked behind the wide trunk of an old tree near the pavement. Her heart began to pound as she spied on them.

Neither boy had bothered to put on a real costume. Chuck had a red bandanna tied around his head and a black mask over his eyes. Steve had blackened his cheeks and forehead with big smudges and wore an old tennis hat and a torn raincoat.

Is he supposed to be a tramp? Carly Beth wondered.

She watched them sift through their bags. They had been out for quite a while, she saw. Their bags looked pretty full.

Suddenly, Steve glanced up in her direction.

Carly Beth jerked her head back behind a tree trunk.

Had he seen her?

No.

Don't blow it now, she told herself. You've waited so long for this moment. You've waited so long to pay them back for all the scares.

Carly Beth watched the two boys make their way up to the front porch of the next house. Nearly tripping over the broomstick, she darted away from the tree. She ran across the street and ducked low behind a hedge.

When they come back down the drive, I'll leap out. I'll pounce on them. I'll scare them to death, she thought.

The low hedge smelled piney and sweet. It was still wet from the morning's rain. The wind made the leaves tremble. What was that strange whistling sound?

It took Carly Beth a while to realize it was her own breathing.

She suddenly began to have doubts.

This isn't going to work, she thought, crouching lower behind the trembling hedge.

I am a complete jerk. Chuck and Steve aren't going to be scared by a stupid mask.

I'm going to jump out at them, and they're going to laugh at me. As they always do.

They're going to laugh and say, "Oh, hi, Carly Beth. Looking good!" Or something like that.

And then they'll tell everyone at school how I thought I was so scary and how they ignored me immediately and what a total jerk I am. And everyone will have a good laugh at my expense.

Why did I ever think this would work? What made me think it was such a great idea?

Crouched behind the hedge, Carly Beth could feel her anger grow. Anger at herself. Anger at the two boys.

Her face felt burning hot inside the ugly mask. Her heart thudded loudly. Her rapid breaths whistled against the flat nose.

Chuck and Steve were approaching. She could hear their trainers crunch over the gravel drive.

Carly Beth tensed her leg muscles and prepared to pounce.

Okay, she thought, taking a deep breath, here goes!

It all seemed to happen in slow motion.

The two boys moved slowly past the hedge. They were talking excitedly to each other. But to Carly Beth, their voices seemed low and far away.

She pulled herself up, stepped out from the hedge, and screamed at the top of her lungs.

Even in the dim light, she could see their reactions clearly.

Their eyes went wide. Their mouths dropped open. Their hands shot up above their heads.

Steve cried out. Chuck grabbed the sleeve of Steve's coat.

Carly Beth's scream echoed over the dark front lawn. The sound seemed to hover in the air.

Everything moved so slowly. So slowly, Carly Beth could see Chuck's eyebrows quiver. She could see his chin tremble.

She could see the fear shimmer in Steve's eyes

as they moved from her mask up to the head on the broomstick.

She waved the broomstick menacingly.

Steve uttered a frightened whimper.

Chuck gaped at Carly Beth, his frightened eyes locked on hers. "Carly Beth—is that *you*?" he finally managed to choke out.

Carly Beth uttered an animal growl, but didn't reply.

"Who *are* you?" Steve demanded, his voice trembling.

"It—it's Carly Beth—I think!" Chuck told him. "Is it you in there, Carly Beth?"

Steve let out a tense laugh. "You—scared us!"

"Carly Beth—is it you?" Chuck demanded again.

Carly Beth waved the broomstick. She pointed up to the head. "That's Carly Beth's head," she told them. Her voice was a deep, throaty rasp.

"Huh?" Both boys gazed up at it uncertainly.

"That's Carly Beth's head," she repeated slowly, waving it towards them. The painted eyes of the sculpted face appeared to glare down at them. "Poor Carly Beth didn't want to give up her head tonight. But I took it anyway."

Both boys stared up at the head.

Chuck continued to grip Steve's coatsleeve.

Steve uttered another tense laugh. He stared at Carly Beth, his expression confused. "You're

81

Carly Beth, right? How are you making that weird voice?"

"That's your friend Carly Beth," she growled, pointing up to the head on the broomstick. "That's all that's left of her!"

Chuck swallowed hard. His eyes were trained on the bobbing head. Steve stared intently at Carly Beth's mask.

"Hand over your sweets," Carly Beth snarled, surprised by the vicious tone in her voice.

"Huh?" Steve cried.

"Hand them over. Now. Or I'll put your heads on the stick!"

Both boys laughed, shrill giggles.

"I'm not joking!" Carly Beth roared.

Her angry words cut their laughter short.

"Carly Beth—give us a break," Chuck muttered uncertainly, his eyes still narrowed in fear.

"Yeah. Really," Steve said softly.

"Hand over your bags," Carly Beth insisted coldly. "Or your heads will adorn my stick."

She lowered the broomstick towards them menacingly.

And as she lowered it, all three of them stared up at the dark-eyed face. All three of them studied the frozen face, the face that looked so real, that looked so much like Carly Beth Caldwell.

A sudden breeze swirled around them, making the head bob on the stick.

And then, all three of them saw the eyes blink. Once. Twice.

The brown eyes blinked.

And the lips on the head parted, making a dry scraping sound.

Frozen in horror, Carly Beth stared up at the face along with the two boys.

And all three of them saw the lips move. And heard the dry, crackling sound.

All three of them saw the dark lips squeeze together, then apart.

All three of them saw the bobbing head form the silent words: *"Help me. Help me."*

In her horror, Carly Beth let go of the broom-stick. It hit the ground beside Chuck. The head rolled under the hedge.

"It—it *talked*!" Steve cried.

Chuck uttered a low whimper.

Without another word, both boys dropped their bags of sweets and took off, their trainers thudding loudly on the pavement.

The wind swirled around Carly Beth as if holding her in place.

She felt like tossing her head back and howling.

She felt like tearing off her coat and flying through the night.

She felt like climbing a tree, leaping onto a roof, roaring up at the starless, black sky.

She stood frozen for a long moment, letting the wind sweep around her. The boys had gone. They had fled in terror.

Terror!

84

Carly Beth had succeeded. She had scared them nearly to death.

She knew she'd never forget the horrified looks on their faces, the fear and disbelief that glowed in their dark eyes.

And she would never forget her feeling of triumph. The thrilling sweetness of revenge.

For a brief moment, she realized, she had felt the fear, too.

She had imagined that the head on the stick had come to life, had blinked its eyes, had spoken silently to them.

For a brief moment, she had caught the fear. She had fallen under the spell of her own trickery.

But, of course, the head couldn't come alive, she assured herself now. Of course the lips hadn't moved, hadn't made their silent plea: "*Help me. Help me.*"

It had to be shadows, she knew. Shadows cast by the light of the moon, floating out from behind the shifting, black clouds.

Where was the head?

Where was the broomstick she had dropped?

It didn't matter now. They were no longer of any use to her.

Carly Beth had won her victory.

And now she was running. Running wildly over the front lawns. Jumping over shrubs and hedges. Flying over the dark, hard ground.

She was running blindly, the houses whirring past on both sides. The blustery wind swirled, and she swirled with it, rising over the pavement, rushing through tall weeds, blowing with the wind like a helpless leaf.

Holding her bulging bag of sweets, she ran past startled trick-or-treaters, past glowing pumpkins, past rattling skeletons.

She ran until her breath gave out.

Then she stopped, panting loudly, and shut her eyes, waiting for her heart to stop pounding, for the blood to stop pulsing at her temples.

And a hand grabbed her shoulder roughly from behind.

Startled, Carly Beth shrieked and spun round. "Sabrina!" she cried breathlessly.

Grinning, Sabrina let go of her shoulder. "I've been looking for you for hours," Sabrina scolded. "Where'd you go?"

"I—I think I got lost," Carly Beth replied, still struggling to catch her breath.

"One minute you were there. The next minute, you'd disappeared," Sabrina said, adjusting her mask over her dark hair.

"How'd you do?" Carly Beth asked, trying to speak in her normal voice.

"I ripped my catsuit," Sabrina complained, frowning. She pulled at the Lycra material on one leg to show Carly Beth. "Snagged it on a stupid letterbox."

"Bad news," Carly Beth sympathized.

"Did you scare anyone with that mask?" Sabrina demanded, still fingering the tear in the catsuit leg.

"Yeah. A few kids," Carly Beth replied casually.

"It's really gross," Sabrina said.

"That's why I chose it."

They both laughed.

"Did you get a lot of sweets?" Sabrina asked. She picked up Carly Beth's bag and looked inside. "Wow! What a haul!"

"I hit a lot of houses," Carly Beth said.

"Let's go back to my house and check out the loot," Sabrina suggested.

"Yeah. Okay." Carly Beth followed her friend across the street.

"Unless you want to trick-or-treat some more," Sabrina offered, stopping in the middle of the street.

"No. I've done enough," Carly Beth said. She laughed to herself. *I did everything I wanted to do tonight.*

They started walking again. They were walking against the wind, but Carly Beth didn't feel at all chilled.

Two girls in frilly dresses, their faces brightly made up, funny, blonde, mop-like wigs on their heads, ran by. One of them slowed when she caught sight of Carly Beth's mask. She uttered a soft gasp, then hurried after her friend.

"Did you see Steve and Chuck?" Sabrina asked. "I searched everywhere for them." She groaned. "That's all I did tonight. I spent the whole night looking for everybody. You. Steve and Chuck. How come we never got together?"

Carly Beth shrugged. "I saw them," she told her friend. "A few minutes ago. Back there." She motioned with her head. "They're such scaredy-cats."

"Huh? Steve and Chuck?" Sabrina's expression turned to surprise.

"Yeah. They got one look at my mask and they took off," Carly Beth told her, laughing. "They were screaming like babies."

Sabrina joined in the laughter. "I don't believe it!" she exclaimed. "They always act so tough. And—"

"I called after them, but they just kept running," Carly Beth told her, grinning.

"Weird!" Sabrina declared.

"Yeah. Weird," Carly Beth agreed.

"Did they know it was you?" Sabrina asked.

Carly Beth shrugged. "I don't know. They took one look at me, and they ran like rabbits."

"They told me they planned to scare *you*," Sabrina revealed. "They were going to sneak up behind you and make scary noises or something."

Carly Beth sniggered. "It's hard to sneak up behind someone when you're running for your life!"

Sabrina's house came into view. Carly Beth shifted the bag of sweets to her other hand.

"I got some good stuff," Sabrina said, peering into her bag as she walked. "I had to get a lot. I have to share it with my cousin. She has the 'flu and couldn't trick-or-treat tonight."

"I'm not sharing any of mine," Carly Beth said. "Noah went out with his pals. He'll probably come home with a year's supply."

"Mrs Connelly gave cookies and popcorn again this year," Sabrina said, sighing. "I'll just have to throw it all out. Mum won't let me eat anything that isn't wrapped. She's afraid some ghoul will put poison in it. I had to throw out a lot of good stuff last year."

Sabrina knocked on her front door. A few seconds later, her mother opened it and the girls entered. "That's some mask, Carly Beth," Sabrina's mum said, studying it. "How'd you girls do?"

"Okay, I think," Sabrina replied.

"Well, just remember—"

"I know. I know, Mum," Sabrina interrupted impatiently. "Throw out everything that isn't wrapped. Even the fruit."

As soon as Mrs Mason had gone back to the study, the two girls emptied out their bags, dumping all the sweets onto the living room carpet.

"Hey, look—a big Milky Way!" Sabrina declared, pulling it out of the pile. "My favourite!"

"I *hate* these!" Carly Beth said, holding up an

enormous blue liquorice lace. "The last time I tried sucking one of these, I turned my tongue bright blue." She tossed it onto Sabrina's pile.

"Thanks a lot," Sabrina said sarcastically. She tugged off her mask and dropped it onto the carpet. Her face was flushed. She shook out her black hair.

"There. That feels better," Sabrina said. "Wow. That mask was hot." She raised her eyes to Carly Beth. "Don't you want to take off your mask? You must be *boiling* inside it!"

"Yeah. Good idea." Carly Beth had actually forgotten she was wearing a mask.

She reached up with both hands and tugged at the ears. "Ouch!" The mask didn't budge.

She pulled it by the top of the head. Then she tried stretching it out and tugging it from the cheeks.

"Ouch!"

"What's wrong?" Sabrina asked, concentrating on sorting her sweets into piles.

Carly Beth didn't reply. She tried prising the mask off at her neck. Then she tugged it up by the ears again.

"Carly Beth—what's wrong?" Sabrina asked, looking up from her sweets.

"Help me!" Carly Beth pleaded in a shrill, frightened voice. "Please—help me! The mask—it won't come off!"

91

On her knees on the carpet, Sabrina glanced up from her piles of chocolate bars. "Carly Beth, stop clowning around."

"I'm not!" Carly Beth insisted, her voice shrill with panic.

"Aren't you tired of scaring people tonight?" Sabrina demanded. She picked up a clear plastic bag of corn chips. "Wonder if Mum will let me keep this. It's wrapped."

"I'm not trying to scare you. I'm serious!" Carly Beth cried. She tugged at the ears of the mask, but couldn't get a good grip.

Sabrina tossed down the bag of corn chips and climbed to her feet. "You really can't get the mask off?"

Carly Beth pulled hard on the chin. "Ouch!" she cried out in pain. "It—it's stuck to my skin or something. Help me."

Sabrina laughed. "We're going to look pretty stupid if we have to call the fire brigade to get you out of your mask!"

Carly Beth didn't find it funny. She gripped the top of the mask with both hands and pulled with all her strength. The mask didn't budge.

Sabrina's grin faded. She stepped over to her friend. "You're not teasing—*are* you? You're really stuck."

Carly Beth nodded. "Well, come on," she urged impatiently. "Help me pull it off."

Sabrina grabbed the mask top. "It's so warm!" she exclaimed. "You must be suffocating in there."

"Just pull!" Carly Beth wailed.

Sabrina pulled.

"Ouch! Not so hard!" Carly Beth cried. "It really hurts!"

Sabrina pulled more gently, but the mask didn't budge. She lowered her hands to the cheeks and pulled.

"Ouch!" Carly Beth shrieked. "It's really stuck to my face."

"What's this thing made of?" Sabrina asked, staring intently at the mask. "It doesn't feel like rubber. It feels like skin."

"I don't know what it's made of, and I don't care," Carly Beth grumbled. "I just want it off. Maybe we should cut it off. You know. With scissors."

"And wreck the mask?" Sabrina asked.

"I don't care!" Carly Beth exclaimed, tugging

furiously at it. "I really don't! I just want out! If I don't get this thing off me, I'm going to freak out. I'm serious!"

Sabrina put a calming hand on her friend's shoulder. "Okay. Okay. One more try. Then we'll cut it off."

She narrowed her eyes as she examined the mask. "I should be able to reach underneath it and pull it away," she said, thinking out loud. "If I slip my hands up through the neck, I can stretch it out and then push it up."

"Well, go ahead. Just hurry!" Carly Beth pleaded.

But Sabrina didn't move. Her dark eyes grew wide, and her mouth dropped open as she studied the mask. She uttered a soft gasp of surprise.

"Sabrina? What's the matter?" Carly Beth demanded.

Sabrina didn't reply. Instead, she ran her fingers over Carly Beth's throat.

Her astonished expression remained frozen on her face. She moved behind Carly Beth and ran her fingers along the back of Carly Beth's neck.

"What *is* it? What's the matter?" Carly Beth demanded shrilly.

Sabrina ran a hand back through her black hair. Her forehead wrinkled in concentration. "Carly Beth," she said finally, "there's something very weird going on here."

"What? What are you *talking* about?" Carly Beth demanded.

"There's no bottom to the mask."

"Huh?" Carly Beth's hands shot up to her neck. She felt around frantically. "What do you *mean*?"

"There's no line," Sabrina told her in a trembling voice. "There's no line between the mask and your skin. No place to slip my hand in."

"But that's crazy!" Carly Beth cried. She moved her hands to her throat, pushing up the skin, feeling for the bottom of the mask. "That's crazy! Just crazy!"

Sabrina raised her hands to her face, her features tight with horror.

"That's crazy! Crazy!" Carly Beth repeated in a high-pitched, frightened voice.

But as her trembling fingers desperately explored her neck, Carly Beth realized that her friend was right.

There was no longer a bottom to the mask. No place where the mask ended. No opening between the mask and Carly Beth's skin.

The mask had become her face.

Carly Beth's legs trembled as she made her way to the mirror by the front door. Her hands still frantically searched her throat as she stepped up to the large, rectangular wall mirror and brought her face close to the glass.

"No line!" she cried. "No mask line!"

Sabrina stood a few metres back, her expression troubled. "I—I don't understand it," she muttered, staring at Carly Beth's reflection.

Carly Beth uttered a sharp gasp. "Those aren't my eyes!" she screamed.

"Huh?" Sabrina stepped up beside her, still staring into the mirror.

"Those aren't my eyes!" Carly Beth wailed. "My eyes don't look like that."

"Try to calm down," Sabrina urged softly. "Your eyes—"

"They're not mine! Not mine!" Carly Beth cried, ignoring her friend's plea for calm.

"Where are my eyes? Where am *I*? Where am I, Sabrina? This isn't *me* in here!"

"Carly Beth—please calm down!" Sabrina urged. But her voice came out choked and frightened.

"It isn't me!" Carly Beth declared, gaping in open-mouthed horror at her reflection, her hands pressed tightly against the grotesquely wrinkled cheeks of the mask. "It isn't me!"

Sabrina reached out to her friend. But Carly Beth pulled away. With a high-pitched wail, a cry of horror and despair, she flung herself through the hallway. She pulled open the front door, struggling with the lock, sobbing loudly.

"Carly Beth—stop! Come back!"

Ignoring Sabrina's pleas, Carly Beth plunged back into the darkness. The screen door slammed behind her.

As she began to run, she could hear Sabrina's frantic cries from the doorway: "Carly Beth— your coat! Come back! You forgot your coat!"

Carly Beth's trainers thudded over the hard ground. She ran into the darkness beneath the trees, as if trying to hide, as if trying to keep her hideous face from view.

She reached the pavement, turned right, and kept running.

She had no idea where she was going. She only

knew she had to run away from Sabrina, away from the mirror.

She wanted to run away from *herself*, away from her face, the hideous face that had stared back at her in the mirror with those frightening, unfamiliar eyes.

Someone else's eyes. Someone else's eyes in her head.

Only it was no longer her head. It was an ugly green monster head that had attached itself to hers.

Uttering another cry of panic, Carly Beth crossed the street and kept running. The dark trees, black against the starless night sky, swayed and shivered overhead. Houses whirred past, a blur of orange light from their windows.

Into the darkness she ran, breathing noisily through the ugly, flat nose. She lowered her smooth, green head against the wind and stared at the ground as she ran.

But no matter where she turned her gaze, she saw the mask. She saw the face staring back at her, the ugly, puckered skin, the glowing orange eyes, the rows of jagged animal teeth.

My face . . . my face . . .

High-pitched screams startled her from her thoughts.

Carly Beth glanced up to see that she had run into a group of trick-or-treaters. There were six or seven of them, all turned towards her, screaming and pointing.

She opened her mouth wide, revealing the sharp fangs, and growled at them, a deep animal growl.

The growl made them grow silent. They stared hard at her, trying to decide if she was threatening them or only kidding.

"What are *you* supposed to be?" a girl in a red-and-white ruffled clown costume called to her.

I'm supposed to be ME, but I'm not! Carly Beth thought bitterly.

She ignored the question. Lowering her head, turning away from them, she started to run again.

She could hear them laughing now. They were laughing in relief, she knew, glad she was leaving them.

With a bitter sob, she turned the corner and kept running.

Where am I going? What am I doing? Am I going to keep running forever?

The questions roared through her mind.

She stopped short when the party shop came into view.

Of course, she thought. The party shop.

The strange man in the cape. He will help me. He will know what to do.

The man in the cape will know how to get this mask off.

99

Feeling a surge of hope, Carly Beth jogged towards the shop.

But as she neared it, her hope dimmed as dark as the shop window. Through the glass she could see that all the lights were out. The shop was as dark as the night. It was closed.

As she stared into the darkened shop, a wave of despair swept over Carly Beth.

Her hands raised against the window, she pressed her head against the glass. It felt cool against her hot forehead. The *mask's* hot forehead.

She closed her eyes.

What do I do now? What am I going to do?

"It's all a bad dream," she murmured out loud. "A bad dream. I'm going to open my eyes now, and wake up."

She opened her eyes. She could see her eyes, her glowing orange eyes, reflected in the dark window glass.

She could see her grotesque face, staring darkly back at her.

"Nooo!" With a shudder that shook her whole body, Carly Beth slammed her fists against the window.

Why didn't I wear my mother's duck costume?

she asked herself angrily. Why was I so determined to be the scariest creature that ever roamed on Hallowe'en? Why was I so determined to terrify Chuck and Steve?

She swallowed hard. Now I'm going to scare people for the rest of my life.

As the bitter thoughts rolled through her mind, Carly Beth suddenly became aware of movement inside the shop. She saw a dark shadow roll over the floor. She heard footsteps.

The door rattled, then opened a few centimetres.

The shop owner poked his head out. His eyes narrowed as they studied Carly Beth. "I stayed late," he said quietly. "I expected to see you again."

Carly Beth was startled by his calmness. "I—I can't get it off!" she spluttered. She tugged at the top of her head to demonstrate.

"I know," the man said. His expression didn't change. "Come inside." He pushed the door open the rest of the way, then stepped back.

Carly Beth hesitated, then walked quickly into the dark shop. It was very warm inside.

The owner turned on a single light above the front counter. He was no longer wearing the cape, Carly Beth saw. He wore black suit trousers and a white dress shirt.

"You *knew* I'd come back?" Carly Beth

102

demanded shrilly. The raspy voice she had acquired inside the mask revealed both anger and confusion. "How did you know?"

"I didn't want to sell it to you," he replied, staring at the mask. He shook his head, frowning. "You remember, don't you? You remember that I didn't want to sell it to you?"

"I remember," Carly Beth replied impatiently. "Just help me take it off. Okay? Help me."

He stared hard at her. He didn't reply.

"Help me take it off," Carly Beth insisted, shouting. "I want you to take it off!"

He sighed. "I can't," he told her sadly. "I can't take it off. I'm really sorry."

"Wh-what do you mean?" Carly Beth stammered.

The shop owner didn't reply. He turned towards the back of the shop and motioned for her to follow him.

"Answer me!" Carly Beth shrieked. "Don't walk away! Answer me! What do you *mean* the mask can't be taken off?"

She followed him into the back room, her heart pounding. He clicked on the light.

Carly Beth blinked in the sudden brightness. The two long shelves of hideous masks came into focus. She saw a bare spot on the shelf where hers had stood.

The grotesque masks all seemed to stare at her. She forced herself to look away from them. "Take this mask off—now!" she demanded, moving to block the shop owner's path.

"I can't remove it," he repeated softly, almost sadly.

"Why not?" Carly Beth demanded.

He lowered his voice. "Because it isn't a mask."

Carly Beth gaped at him. She opened her mouth, but no sound came out.

"It isn't a mask," he told her. "It's a real face."

Carly Beth suddenly felt dizzy. The floor tilted. The rows of ugly faces glared at her. All of the bulging, bloodshot, yellow and green eyes seemed to be trained on her.

She pressed her back against the wall and tried to steady herself.

The shop owner walked over to the display shelf and gestured to the ugly, staring heads. "The Unloved," he said sadly, his voice lowered to a whisper.

"I—I don't understand," Carly Beth managed to choke out.

"These are not masks. They are faces," he explained. "Real faces. I made them. I created them in my lab—real faces."

"But—but they are so ugly—" Carly Beth started. "Why—?"

"They weren't ugly in the beginning," he interrupted, his voice bitter, his eyes angry. "They were beautiful. And they were alive. But something went wrong. When they were taken out of the lab, they changed. My experiments— my poor heads—were a failure. But I had to keep them alive. I *had* to."

105

"I—I don't believe it!" Carly Beth exclaimed breathlessly, raising her hands to the sides of her face, her green, distorted face. "I don't believe any of it."

"I am telling the truth," the shop owner continued, running a finger over one side of his narrow moustache, his eyes burning into Carly Beth's. "I keep them here. I call them The Unloved because no one will ever want to see them. Occasionally, someone wanders into the back room—you, for example—and one of my faces finds a new home. . . ."

"*Nooooo!*" Carly Beth uttered a cry of protest, more an animal wail than a human cry.

She stared at the gnarled, twisted faces on the shelf. The bulging heads, the open wounds, the animal fangs. Monsters! All monsters!

"Take this off!" she screamed, losing control. "Take this off! Take it off!"

She began tearing frantically at her face, trying to pull it off, trying to rip it off in pieces.

"Take it off! Take it off!"

He raised a hand to calm her. "I am sorry. The face is your face now," he said without expression.

"No!" Carly Beth shrieked again in her new, raspy voice. "Take it off! Take it off!—NOW!"

She tore at the face. But even in her anger and panic, she knew her actions were useless.

"The face can be removed," the shop owner told her, speaking softly.

"Huh?" Carly Beth lowered her hands. She stared hard at him. "What did you say?"

"I said there is one way the face can be removed."

"Yes?" Carly Beth felt a powerful chill run down her back, a chill of hope. "Yes? How? Tell me!" she pleaded. "Please—tell me!"

"I cannot do it for you," he replied, frowning. "But I can tell you how. However, if it ever again attaches itself to you or to another person, it will be forever."

"How do I get it off? Tell me! *Tell me!*" Carly Beth begged. "How do I get it off?"

The light flickered overhead. The rows of bloated, distorted faces continued to stare at Carly Beth.

Monsters, she thought.

It's a room full of monsters, waiting to come alive.

And now I'm one of them.

Now I'm a monster, too.

The floorboards creaked as the shop owner moved away from the display shelves and came up close to Carly Beth.

"How do I get this off me?" she pleaded. "Tell me. Show me—now!"

"It can only be removed once," he repeated softly. "And it can only be removed by a symbol of love."

She stared at him, waiting for him to continue.

The silence filled the room. Heavy silence.

"I—I don't understand," Carly Beth stammered firmly. "You've *got* to help me. I don't understand you! Tell me something that makes sense! *Help* me!"

"I can say no more," he said, lowering his head, shutting his eyes, and wearily rubbing his eyelids with his fingers.

"But—what do you *mean* by a symbol of love?" Carly Beth demanded. She grabbed the front of his shirt with both hands. "What do you mean? *What do you mean?*"

He made no attempt to remove her hands. "I can say no more," he repeated in a whisper.

"No!" she shouted. "No! You *have* to help me! You *have* to!"

She could feel her rage explode, could feel herself burst out of control—but she couldn't stop herself.

"I want my face back!" she shrieked, pounding on his chest with both fists. "I want my face back! I want *myself* back!"

She was screaming at the top of her lungs now, but she didn't care.

The shop owner backed away, motioning with both hands for her to be quiet. Then, suddenly, his eyes opened wide in fear.

Carly Beth followed his gaze to the display shelves.

"Ohh!" She uttered a startled cry of horror as she saw the rows of faces all begin to move.

Bulging eyes blinked. Swollen tongues licked at dry lips. Dark wounds began to pulsate.

The heads were all bobbing, blinking, *breathing*.

"What—what is happening?" Carly Beth cried in a trembling whisper.

"You've awakened them all!" he cried, his expression as frightened as hers.

"But—but—"

"Run!" he screamed, giving her a hard shove towards the doorway. "Run!"

Carly Beth hesitated. She turned back to stare at the heads bobbing on the shelves.

Fat, dark lips began to move, making wet sucking sounds. Crooked fangs clicked up and down. Ugly, inhuman noses twitched and gasped air noisily.

The heads, two long rows of them, throbbed to life.

And the eyes—the blood-veined, bulging eyes—the green eyes, the sickly yellow eyes, the bright scarlet eyes, the disgusting eyeballs hanging by threads—*they were all on her!*

"Run! You've awakened them!" the shop owner screamed, his voice choked with fear. "Run! Get *away* from here!"

Carly Beth wanted to run. But her legs wouldn't cooperate. Her knees felt wobbly and weak. She suddenly felt as if she weighed a thousand kilos.

"Run! *Run!*" The shop owner repeated his frantic cry.

But she couldn't take her eyes off the throbbing, twitching heads.

Carly Beth gaped at the hideous scene, frozen in terror, feeling her legs turn to jelly, feeling her breath catch in her throat. And as she watched, the heads rose up and floated into the air.

"Run! Hurry! Run!"

The shop owner's voice seemed far away now.

The heads began to jabber in rumbling, deep voices, drowning out his frantic cries. They murmured excitedly, making only sounds, no words, like a chorus of frogs.

Up, up, they floated, as Carly Beth stared in silent horror.

"Run! Run!"

Yes.

She turned. She forced her legs to move.

And with a burst of energy, she began to run.

She ran through the dimly lit front room of the shop. Her hands grabbed for the doorknob, and she pulled open the door.

A second later, she was out on the pavement, running through the darkness. Her shoes thudded loudly on the ground. She felt a shock of cold air against her hot face.

Her hot, green face.

Her monster face.

The monster face she could not remove.

She crossed the street and kept running.

What was that sound? That deep, gurgling sound? That low murmur that seemed to be following her?

Following her?

"Oh, no!" Carly Beth cried out as she glanced back—and saw the gruesome heads flying after her.

A ghoulish parade.

They flew in single file, one long chain of throbbing, jabbering heads. Their eyes glowed brightly, as bright as car headlights, and they were all trained on Carly Beth.

Choked with fear, Carly Beth stumbled over the kerb.

Her arms shot forward as she struggled to regain her balance. Her legs wanted to collapse, but she forced them to move again.

Bent into the wind, she ran, past dark houses and empty alleyways.

It must be late, she realized. It must be very late.

Too late.

The words flashed into her mind.

Too late for me.

The hideous, glowing heads flew after her. Getting closer. Closer. The rumbling of their animal murmurs grew louder in her ears until the frightening sound seemed to surround her.

The wind roared, gusting hard, as if deliberately pushing her back.

The murmuring heads floated closer.

I'm running through a dark nightmare, she thought.

I may run forever.

Too late. Too late for me.

Or *was* it?

An idea formed its way through her nightmarish panic. As she ran, her arms thrashing the air in front of her as if reaching for safety, her mind struggled for a solution, an escape.

A *symbol of love*.

She heard the shop owner's words over the rumble of ugly voices behind her.

A *symbol of love*.

That's what it would take to rid her of the monster head that had become her own.

Would it also stop the throbbing, glowing heads that pursued her? Would it send the faces of The Unloved back to where they came from?

Gasping loudly for breath, Carly Beth turned the corner and kept running. Glancing back, she could see her chattering pursuers turn, too.

Where *am* I? she wondered, turning her eyes to the houses she was passing.

She had been too frightened to care where she ran.

But, now, Carly Beth had an idea. A desperate idea.

And she had to get there before the gruesome parade of heads caught up with her.

She *had* a symbol of love.

It was her head. The plaster of Paris head her mother had sculpted of her.

Carly Beth remembered asking her mother why she had sculpted it. And her mother had replied, "Because I love you." Maybe it could save her. Maybe it could help her out of this nightmare.

But where was it?

She had tossed it aside. She had let it fall behind a hedge. She had left it in someone's garden, and—

And now she was back on the street.

She recognized the street. She recognized the houses.

This was where she had met up with Chuck and Steve. This was where she had sent them running off in terror.

But where was the house? Where was the hedge?

Her eyes darted frantically from garden to garden.

Behind her, she saw, the heads had swarmed together. Like buzzing bees, they had bunched together, grinning now, grinning hideous, wet grins as they prepared to close in on her.

I've got to find the head! Carly Beth told herself, struggling to breathe, struggling to keep her aching legs moving.

I've got to find my head.

The rumbling, jabbering voices grew louder. The heads swarmed closer.

"Where? Where?" she screamed aloud.

And then she saw the tall hedge. Across the street.

The garden across the street.

The head, the beautiful head—she had let it fall behind that hedge.

Could she get to it before the ugly heads swarmed over her?

Yes!

Sucking in a deep breath of air, her arms reaching out desperately in front of her, she turned and ran across the street.

And dived behind the hedge. On to her hands and knees. Her chest heaving. Her breath rasping. Her head pounding.

She reached for the head.

It had gone.

Gone.

The head had gone.

My last chance, Carly Beth thought, searching blindly, her hand thrashing frantically through the bottom of the hedge.

Gone.

Too late for me.

Still on her knees, she turned to face her ghoulish pursuers. The heads, jabbering their mindless sounds, rose up in front of her, forming a wall.

Carly Beth started to her feet.

The throbbing wall of monster heads inched closer.

She turned, searching for an escape route.

And saw it.

Saw her head.

Saw the plaster of Paris head staring up at her from between two upraised roots on the big tree near the drive.

The wind must have blown it over there, she realized.

And as the ugly heads bobbed closer, she dived for the tree. And grabbed the head with both hands.

With a cry of triumph, she turned the sculpted face towards the jabbering heads and raised it high.

"Go away! Go away!" Carly Beth screamed, holding the head up so they could all see it. "This is a symbol of love! This is a symbol of love! Go away!"

The heads bobbed together. The glowing eyes stared at the sculpted head.

They murmured excitedly. Wet smiles formed on their distorted lips.

"Go away! Go away!"

Carly Beth heard them laugh. Low, scornful laughter.

Then they moved quickly, surrounding her, eager to swallow her up.

Too late for me.

The words repeated in Carly Beth's mind.

Her idea had failed.

The heads swarmed around her, drooled over her, eyes bulging gleefully in triumph.

Their rumbling murmurs became a roar. She felt herself being swallowed up in their foul-smelling heat.

Without thinking, she lowered the sculpted head. And pulled it down hard over her hideous monster head.

To her surprise, it slid over her like a mask.

I'm wearing my own face like a mask, she thought bitterly.

As she pulled it over her, darkness descended.

There were no eyeholes. She couldn't see out.

She couldn't hear.

What will the gruesome heads do to me? she wondered, alone with her fear.

Will I become one of The Unloved now?

119

Will I end up on display on a shelf along with them?

Surrounded by the tight, silent darkness, Carly Beth waited.

And waited.

She could feel the blood pulsing at her temples. She could feel the throb of fear in her chest, the ache of her dry throat.

What are they going to do?

What are they *doing*?

She couldn't bear being alone, shut in with her fear, surrounded by silence and the dark.

With a hard tug, she pulled off the sculpted head.

The gruesome heads had gone.

Vanished.

Carly Beth stared straight ahead in disbelief. Then her eyes darted around the shadowy lawn. She searched the trees and shrubs. She squinted into the dark spaces between the houses.

Gone.

They had gone.

For a long moment, Carly Beth sat in the cold, wet grass, the sculpted head on her lap, breathing hard, staring across the silent, empty front garden.

Soon her breathing returned to normal. She climbed to her feet.

The wind had gentled. The pale half-moon

slipped out from behind the dark clouds that had covered it.

Carly Beth felt something flap against her throat.

Startled, she reached up and felt the bottom of the mask.

The bottom of the mask?

Yes!

There was a gap between the mask and her neck.

"Hey!" she cried aloud. Putting the sculpted head down gently at her feet, she raised both hands to the bottom of the mask and pulled up.

The mask came off easily.

Stunned, she lowered it and held it in front of her. She folded it up, then unfolded it.

The orange eyes that had glowed like fire had faded. The pointed animal fangs had become rubbery and limp.

"You're just a mask!" she cried aloud. "Just a mask again!"

Laughing gleefully, she tossed it up in the air and caught it.

It can be removed only once, the shop owner had told her.

Only once by a symbol of love.

Well, I've done it! Carly Beth told herself happily. I've removed it. And don't worry—I'll never put it on again!

Never!

121

She suddenly felt exhausted.

I've got to get home, she told herself. It's probably close to midnight.

Most of the houses were dark. There were no cars moving on the streets. The trick-or-treaters had all gone home.

Carly Beth bent to pick up the sculpted head. Then, carrying the mask and the plaster head, she began walking quickly towards her house.

Halfway up the drive, she stopped.

She reached up and examined her face with one hand.

Do I have my old face back? she wondered.

She rubbed her cheeks, then ran her fingers over her nose.

Is it my old face? Do I look like me?

She couldn't tell just by touching.

"I've got to get to a mirror!" she exclaimed out loud.

Desperate to see if her face had returned to normal, she ran up to her front door and rang the bell.

After a few seconds the door swung open, and Noah appeared. He pushed open the storm door.

Then he raised his eyes to her face—and started to scream.

"Take off that mask! Take it off! You're so ugly!!"

"No!" Carly Beth cried in horror.

The mask must have changed her face, she realized.

"No! Oh, no!"

She pushed past her brother, tossed down the head and the mask, and ran to the hall mirror.

Her face stared back at her.

Perfectly normal. Her old face. Her good old face.

Her dark brown eyes. Her broad forehead. Her snip of a nose, which she had always wished was longer.

I'll never complain about my nose again, she thought happily.

Her face was normal again. All normal.

As she stared at herself, she could hear Noah laughing in the doorway.

She spun around angrily. "Noah—how *could* you?"

123

He laughed harder. "It was just a joke. I can't believe you fell for it."

"It was no joke to me!" Carly Beth exclaimed angrily.

Her mother appeared at the end of the hall. "Carly Beth, where have you been? I expected you back an hour ago."

"Sorry, Mum," Carly Beth replied, grinning.

I'm so happy, I may never stop grinning! she thought.

"It's sort of a long story," she told her mother. "Sort of a long, weird story."

"But you're okay?" Mrs Caldwell's eyes narrowed as she studied her daughter.

"Yeah. I'm okay," Carly Beth said.

"Come into the kitchen," Mrs Caldwell instructed her. "I have some nice hot cider for you."

Carly Beth obediently followed her mother to the kitchen. The kitchen was warm and bright. The sweet cider aroma filled the room.

Carly Beth had never been so glad to be home in all her life. She hugged her mother, then took a seat at the worktop.

"Why didn't you wear your duck costume?" Mrs Caldwell asked, pouring out a cup of steaming cider. "Where have you been? Why weren't you with Sabrina? Sabrina has phoned twice already, wondering what happened to you."

"Well . . ." Carly Beth began. "It's sort of a long story, Mum."

"I'm not going anywhere," her mother said, putting the cup of cider down in front of Carly Beth. She leaned against the worktop, resting her chin in one hand. "Go ahead. Talk."

"Well . . ." Carly Beth hesitated. "Everything is fine now, Mum. Perfectly fine. But—"

Before she could say another word, Noah burst into the room.

"Hey, Carly Beth—" he called in a deep, raspy voice. "Look at me! How do I look in your mask?"

Piano Lessons Can Be Murder

I thought I was going to hate moving into a new house. But actually, I had fun.

I played a pretty mean joke on Mum and Dad.

While they were busy in the front room showing the removal men where to put stuff, I went exploring. I found a really great room to the side of the dining room.

It had big windows on two sides looking out onto the back garden. Sunlight poured in, making the room brighter and a lot more cheery than the rest of the old house.

The room was going to be our new family room. You know, with a TV and CD player, and maybe a ping-pong table and stuff. But right now it was completely empty.

Except for two grey balls of dust in one corner, which gave me an idea.

Chuckling to myself, I bent down and shaped the two dust balls with my hands. Then I began shouting in a really panicky voice: "Mice! Mice! Help! *Mice!*"

Mum and Dad came bursting into the room at the same time. Their mouths nearly dropped to the floor when they saw the two grey dust mice.

I kept screaming, "Mice! Mice!" Pretending I was scared of them. Trying hard to keep a straight face.

Mum just stood in the doorway, her mouth hanging open. I really thought she was going to drop her teeth!

Dad always panics more than Mum. He picked up a broom that was leaning against the wall, ran across the room, and began pounding the poor, defenceless dust mice with it.

By that time, I was laughing my head off.

Dad stared down at the glob of dust stuck to the end of the broom, and he finally caught on that it was a joke. His face got really red, and I thought his eyes were going to pop out from behind his glasses.

"Very funny, Jerome," Mum said calmly, rolling her eyes. Everyone calls me Jerry, but she calls me Jerome when she's upset with me. "Your father and I certainly appreciate your scaring us to death when we're both very nervous and overworked and trying to get moved into this house."

Mum is always really sarcastic like that. I

think I probably get my sense of humour from her.

Dad just scratched the bald spot on the back of his head. "They really looked like mice," he muttered. He wasn't angry. He's used to my jokes. They both are.

"Why can't you act your age?" Mum asked, shaking her head.

"I am!" I insisted. I mean, I'm twelve. So I *was* acting my age. If you can't play jokes on your parents and try to have a little fun at twelve, when *can* you?

"Don't be such a clever-dick," Dad said, giving me his stern look. "There's a lot of work to be done around here, you know, Jerry. You could help out."

He shoved the broom towards me.

I raised both hands as if shielding myself from danger, and backed away. "Dad, you *know* I'm allergic!" I cried.

"Allergic to dust?" he asked.

"No. Allergic to work!"

I expected them to laugh, but they just stormed out of the room, muttering to themselves. "You can at least look after Bonkers," Mum called back to me. "Keep her out of the removal men's way."

"Yeah. Sure," I called back. Bonkers is our cat, and there's *no way* I can keep Bonkers from doing anything!

Let me say straight away that Bonkers is *not* my favourite member of our family. In fact, I keep as far away from Bonkers as I can.

No one ever explained to the stupid cat that she's supposed to be a pet. Instead, I think Bonkers believes she's a wild, man-eating tiger. Or maybe a vampire bat.

Her favourite trick is to climb up on the back of a chair or a high shelf—and then leap with her claws out onto your shoulders. I can't tell you how many good T-shirts have been ripped to shreds by this trick of hers. Or how much blood I've lost.

The cat isn't nasty—just plain vicious.

She's all black except for a white circle over her forehead and one eye. Mum and Dad think she's just wonderful. They're always picking her up, and petting her, and telling her how adorable she is. Bonkers usually scratches them and makes them bleed. But they never learn.

When we moved to this new house, I was hoping maybe Bonkers would get left behind. But, no way. Mum made sure that Bonkers was in the car first, right next to me.

And of course the stupid cat threw up in the back seat.

Whoever heard of a cat who gets carsick? She did it deliberately because she's horrible and vicious.

Anyway, I ignored Mum's request to keep an eye on her. In fact, I crept into the kitchen and opened the back door, hoping maybe Bonkers would run away and get lost.

Then I continued my exploring.

Our other house was tiny, but new. This house was old. The floorboards creaked. The windows rattled. The house seemed to groan when you walked through it.

But it was really big. I discovered all kinds of little rooms and deep cupboards. One upstairs cupboard was as big as my old bedroom!

My new bedroom was at the end of the passage on the first floor. There were three other rooms and a bathroom up there. I wondered what Mum and Dad planned to do with all those rooms.

I decided to suggest that one of them be made into a Nintendo room. We could put a wide-screen TV in there to play the games on. It would be really great.

As I made plans for my new video game room, I started to feel a little cheered up. I mean, it isn't easy to move to a new house in a new town.

I'm not the kind of kid who cries much. But I have to admit that I felt like crying a *lot* when we moved away from Cedarville. Especially when I had to say goodbye to my friends.

Especially Sean. Sean is a great kid. Mum and Dad don't like him very much because he's kind of noisy and he likes to burp really loud. But Sean is my best friend.

I mean he *was* my best friend.

I don't have any friends here in New Goshen.

Mum said Sean could come and stay with us for a few weeks this summer. That was really nice of her, especially since she hates his burping so much.

But it didn't really cheer me up.

Exploring the new house was making me feel a little better. The room next to mine can be a gym, I decided. We'll get all those great-looking exercise machines they show on TV.

The removal men were hauling stuff into my room, so I couldn't go in there. I pulled open a door to what I thought was a cupboard. But to my surprise, I saw a narrow, wooden staircase. I supposed it led up to an attic.

An attic!

I'd never had an attic before. I bet it's filled with all kinds of great old stuff, I thought excitedly. Maybe the people who used to live here left their old comics collection up there—and it's worth millions!

I was halfway up the stairs when I heard Dad's voice behind me. "Jerry, where are you going?"

"Up," I replied. That was pretty obvious.

"You really shouldn't go up there by yourself," he warned.

"Why not? Are there ghosts up there or something?" I asked.

I could hear his heavy footsteps on the wooden stairs. He followed me up. "Hot up here," he muttered, adjusting his glasses on his nose. "It's so stuffy."

He tugged on a chain suspended from the ceiling, and an overhead light came on, casting pale yellow light down on us.

I glanced quickly around. It was all one room, long and low, the ceiling slanting down on both sides under the roof. I'm not very tall, but I reached up and touched the ceiling.

There were tiny, round windows at both ends. But they were covered with dust and didn't let in much light.

"It's empty," I muttered, very disappointed.

"We can store a lot of junk up here," Dad said, looking around.

"Hey—what's that?" I spotted something against the far wall and began walking quickly towards it. The floorboards squeaked and creaked under my trainers.

I saw a grey, quilted cover over something large. Maybe it's some kind of treasure chest, I thought.

No one could ever accuse me of not having a good imagination.

Dad was right behind me as I grabbed the heavy cover with both hands and pulled it away.

135

And stared at a shiny, black piano.

"Wow," Dad murmured, scratching his bald spot, staring at the piano with surprise. "Wow. Wow. Why did they leave *this* behind?"

I shrugged. "It looks like new," I said. I hit some keys with one finger. "Sounds good."

Dad hit some keys, too. "It's a really good piano," he said, rubbing his hand lightly over the keyboard. "I wonder what it's doing hidden up here in the attic like this. . ."

"It's a mystery," I agreed.

I had no idea how big a mystery it really was.

I couldn't get to sleep that night. I mean, there was no way.

I was in my good old bed from our old house. But it was facing the wrong direction. And it was against a different wall. And the light from the neighbour's back porch was shining through the window. The window rattled from the wind. And all these creepy shadows were moving back and forth across the ceiling.

I'm *never* going to be able to sleep in this new room, I realized.

It's too different. Too creepy. Too big.

I'm going to be awake for the rest of my life!

I just lay there, eyes wide open, staring up at the weird shadows.

136

I had just started to relax and drift off to sleep when I heard the music.

Piano music.

At first, I thought it was coming from outside. But I quickly realized it was coming from up above me. From the attic!

I sat straight up and listened. Yes. Some kind of classical music. Right over my head.

I kicked off the covers and lowered my feet to the floor.

Who could be up in the attic playing the piano in the middle of the night? I wondered. It couldn't be Dad. He can't play a note. And the only thing Mum can play is "Chopsticks", and not very well.

Maybe it's Bonkers, I told myself.

I stood up and listened. The music continued. Very softly. But I could hear it clearly. Every note.

I started to make my way to the door and stubbed my toe against a box that hadn't been unpacked. "Ow!" I cried out, grabbing my foot and hopping around until the pain faded.

Mum and Dad couldn't hear me, I knew. Their bedroom was downstairs.

I held my breath and listened. I could still hear the piano music above my head.

Walking slowly, carefully, I stepped out of my room and into the passage. The floorboards creaked under my bare feet. The floor was cold.

I pulled open the attic door and leaned into the darkness.

The music floated down. It was sad music, very slow, very soft.

"Who—who's up there?" I stammered.

The sad music continued, floating down the dark, narrow stairway to me.

"Who's up there?" I repeated, my voice shaking just a little.

Again, no reply.

I leaned into the darkness, peering up towards the attic. "Mum, is that you? Dad?"

No reply. The melody was so sad, so slow.

Before I even realized what I was doing, I was climbing the stairs. They groaned loudly under my bare feet.

The air grew hot and stuffy as I reached the top of the stairs and stepped into the dark attic.

The piano music surrounded me now. The notes seemed to be coming from all directions at once.

"Who is it?" I demanded in a shrill, high-pitched voice. I suppose I was a little scared. "Who's up here?"

Something brushed against my face, and I nearly jumped out of my skin.

It took me a long, shuddering moment to realize it was the light chain.

I pulled it. Pale yellow light spread out over the long, narrow room.

The music stopped.

"Who's up here?" I called, squinting towards the piano against the far wall.

No one.

No one there. No one sitting at the piano.

Silence.

Except for the floorboards creaking under my feet as I walked over to the piano. I stared at it, stared at the keys.

I don't know what I expected to see. I mean, *someone* was playing the piano. *Someone* played it until the exact second the light went on. Where did they go?

I ducked down and searched under the piano.

I know it was stupid, but I wasn't thinking clearly. My heart was pounding really hard, and all kinds of crazy thoughts were spinning through my brain.

I leaned over the piano and examined the keyboard. I thought maybe this was one of those old-fashioned pianos that played by itself. A player piano. You know, like you sometimes see in cartoons.

But it looked like an ordinary piano. I didn't see anything special about it.

I sat down on the bench.

And jumped up.

The piano bench was warm! As if someone had just been sitting on it!

"Who?" I cried aloud, staring at the shiny, black bench.

I reached down and felt it. It was definitely warm.

But I reminded myself that the whole attic was really warm, much warmer than the rest of the house. The heat seemed to float up here and stay.

I sat back down and waited for my racing heart to return to normal.

What's going on here? I asked myself, turning to stare at the piano. The black wood was polished so well, I could see the reflection of my face staring back at me.

My reflection looked pretty scared.

I lowered my eyes to the keyboard and then hit a few soft notes.

Someone had been playing this piano a few moments ago, I knew.

But how could they have vanished into thin air without me seeing them?

I plunked another note, then another. The sound echoed through the long, empty room.

Then I heard a loud creak. From the bottom of the stairs.

I froze, my hand still on the piano keys.

Another creak. A footstep.

I stood up, surprised to find my legs all trembly.

I listened. I listened so hard, I could hear the air move.

Another footstep. Louder. Closer.

Someone was on the stairs. Someone was climbing to the attic.

Someone was coming for me.

Creak. Creak.

The stairs gave way beneath heavy footsteps.

My breath caught in my throat. I felt as if I would suffocate.

Frozen in front of the piano, I searched for a place to hide. But of course there wasn't any.

Creak. Creak.

And then, as I stared in terror, a head poked up above the staircase.

"Dad!" I cried.

"Jerry, what on earth are you doing up here?" He stepped into the pale yellow light. His thinning brown hair was standing up all over his head. His pyjama bottoms were twisted. One leg had rolled up to the knee. He squinted at me. He didn't have his glasses on.

"Dad—I—I thought—" I spluttered. I knew I sounded like a complete jerk. But give me a break—I was *scared!*

143

"Do you know what time it is?" Dad demanded angrily. He glanced down at his wrist, but he wasn't wearing his watch. "It's the middle of the night, Jerry!"

"I—I know, Dad," I said, starting to feel a little better. I walked over to him. "I heard piano music, you see. And so I thought—"

"You *what?*" His dark eyes grew wide. His mouth dropped open. "You heard *what?*"

"Piano music," I repeated. "Up here. So I came upstairs to check it out, and—"

"Jerry!" Dad exploded. His face got really red. "It's too late for your silly jokes!"

"But, Dad—" I started to protest.

"Your mother and I killed ourselves unpacking and moving furniture all day," Dad said, sighing wearily. "We're both very exhausted, Jerry. I shouldn't have to tell you that I'm in no mood for jokes. I have to go to work tomorrow morning. I need some sleep."

"Sorry, Dad," I said quietly. I could see there was no way I was going to get him to believe me about the piano music.

"I know you're excited about being in a new house," Dad said, putting a hand on the shoulder of my pyjama top. "But, come on. Back to your room. You need your sleep, too."

I glanced back at the piano. It glimmered darkly in the pale yellow light. As if it were breathing. As if it were alive.

I pictured it rumbling towards me, chasing me to the stairs.

Crazy, weird thoughts. I suppose I was more tired than I thought!

"Would you like to learn to play it?" Dad asked suddenly.

"Huh?" His question caught me by surprise.

"Would you like to have piano lessons? We could have the piano brought downstairs. There's room for it in the family room."

"Well . . . maybe," I replied. "Yeah. That might be cool."

He took his hand from my shoulder. Then he straightened his pyjama bottoms and started downstairs. "I'll discuss it with your mother," he said. "I'm sure she'll be pleased. She always wanted someone to be musical in the family. Pull the light chain, okay?"

Obediently, I reached up and clicked off the light. The sudden darkness was so black, it startled me. I stayed close behind my dad as we made our way down the creaking stairs.

Back in my bed, I pulled the covers up to my chin. It was pretty cold in my room. Outside, the winter wind gusted hard. The bedroom window rattled and shook, as if it were shivering.

Piano lessons might be fun, I thought. If they let me learn to play rock music, not that drippy, boring classical stuff.

After a few lessons, maybe I could get a synthesizer. Get two or three different keyboards. Hook them up to a computer.

Then I could do some composing. Maybe get a group together.

Yeah. It could be really excellent.

I closed my eyes.

The window rattled again. The old house seemed to groan.

I'll get used to these noises, I told myself. I'll get used to this old house. After a few nights, I won't even hear the noises.

I had just about drifted off to sleep when I heard the soft, sad piano music begin again.

Monday morning I woke up very early. My cat clock with the moving tail and eyes wasn't unpacked yet. But I could tell it was early by the pale grey light coming through my bedroom window.

I got dressed quickly, pulling on a clean pair of faded jeans and a dark green pullover shirt that wasn't too wrinkled. It was my first day at my new school, so I was pretty excited.

I spent more time on my hair than I usually do. My hair is brown and thick and wiry, and it takes me a long time to slick it down and make it lie flat the way I like it.

When I finally got it right, I made my way down the hall to the front stairs. The house was still silent and dark.

I stopped outside the attic door. It was wide open.

Hadn't I closed it when I'd come downstairs with my dad?

147

Yes. I remembered shutting it tight. And now, here it was, wide open.

I felt a cold chill on the back of my neck. I closed the door, listening for the click.

Jerry, take it easy, I warned myself. Maybe the latch is loose. Maybe the attic door always swings open. It's an old house, remember?

I'd been thinking about the piano music. Maybe it was the wind blowing through the piano strings, I told myself.

Maybe there was a hole or something in the attic window. And the wind blew in and made it sound as if the piano was playing.

I wanted to believe it had been the wind that made that slow, sad music. I wanted to believe it, so I did.

I checked the attic door one more time, making sure it was latched, then headed down to the kitchen.

Mum and Dad were still in their room. I could hear them getting dressed.

The kitchen was dark and a little cold. I wanted to turn up the boiler, but I didn't know where the thermostat was.

Not all of our kitchen stuff had been unpacked. Boxes were still stacked against the wall, filled with glasses and plates and stuff.

I heard someone coming down the hall.

A big, empty packing case beside the fridge gave me an idea. Sniggering to myself, I jumped inside it and pulled the lid over me.

I held my breath and waited.

Footsteps in the kitchen. I couldn't tell if it was Mum or Dad.

My heart was pounding. I continued to hold my breath. If I didn't, I knew I would burst out laughing.

The footsteps went right past my packing case to the sink. I heard water running. Whoever it was had filled the kettle.

Footsteps to the cooker.

I couldn't wait any more.

"*SURPRISE!*" I screamed and jumped to my feet in the packing case.

Dad let out a startled shriek and dropped the kettle. It landed on his foot with a *thud*, then tilted onto its side on the floor.

Water puddled around Dad's feet. The kettle rolled towards the cooker. Dad was howling and holding his injured foot and hopping up and down.

I was laughing like a maniac! You should've seen the look on Dad's face when I jumped up from the case. I really thought he was going to drop his teeth!

Mum came bursting into the room, still buttoning her sleeve cuffs. "What's going on in here?" she cried.

"Just Jerry and his stupid jokes," Dad grumbled.

"Jerome!" Mum shouted, seeing all the spilled water on the lino. "Give us a break."

"Just trying to help wake you up," I said, grinning. They complain a lot, but they're used to my twisted sense of humour.

I heard the piano music again that night.

It was definitely not the wind. I recognized the same sad melody.

I listened for a few moments. It came from right above my room.

Who's up there? Who can be playing? I asked myself.

I started to climb out of bed and investigate. But it was cold in my room, and I was really tired from my first day at the new school.

So I pulled the covers over my head to drown out the piano music, and quickly fell asleep.

"Did you hear the piano music last night?" I asked my mum.

"Eat your cornflakes," she replied. She tightened the belt of her bathrobe and leaned towards me over the kitchen table.

"How come I have to have cornflakes?" I grumbled, mushing the spoon around in the bowl.

"You know the rules," she said, frowning. "Junk cereal only at weekends."

150

"Stupid rule," I muttered. "I think cornflakes is a junk cereal."

"Don't give me a hard time," Mum complained, rubbing her temples. "I have a headache this morning."

"From the piano playing last night?" I asked.

"What piano playing?" she demanded irritably. "Why do you keep talking about piano playing?"

"Didn't you hear it? The piano in the attic? Someone was playing it last night."

She jumped to her feet. "Oh, Jerry, please. No jokes this morning, okay? I told you I have a headache."

"Did I hear you talking about the piano?" Dad came into the kitchen, carrying the morning newspaper. "The men are coming this afternoon to carry it down to the family room." He smiled at me. "Limber up those fingers, Jerry."

Mum had walked over to the worktop to pour herself a cup of coffee. "Are you really interested in this piano?" she demanded, eyeing me sceptically. "Are you really going to practise and work at it?"

"Of course," I replied. "Maybe."

The two piano movers were there when I got home from school. They weren't very big, but they were strong.

151

I went up to the attic and watched them while Mum pulled packing cases out of the family room to make a place for it.

The two men used ropes and a special kind of dolly. They tilted the piano onto its side, then hoisted it onto the dolly.

Lowering it down the narrow staircase was really hard. It bumped against the wall several times, even though they moved slowly and carefully.

Both movers were really red-faced and sweaty by the time they got the piano downstairs. I followed them as they rolled it across the living room, then through the dining room.

Mum came out of the kitchen, her hands jammed into her jeans pockets, and watched from the doorway as they rolled the dolly with the piano into the family room.

The men strained to tilt it right side up. The black, polished wood really glowed in the bright afternoon sunlight through the family room windows.

Then, as they started to lower the piano to the floor, Mum opened her mouth and started to scream.

152

"The cat! The cat!" Mum shrieked, her face all twisted in alarm.

Sure enough, Bonkers was standing right in the spot where they were lowering the piano.

The piano thudded heavily to the floor. Bonkers ran out from under it just in time.

Too bad! I thought, shaking my head. That dumb cat almost got what it deserved.

The men were apologizing as they tried to catch their breath, mopping their foreheads with their handkerchiefs.

Mum ran to Bonkers and picked her up. "My poor little kitty."

Of course Bonkers swiped at Mum's arm, her claws tearing out several threads in the sweater sleeve. Mum dropped her to the floor, and the creature slithered quickly out of the room.

"She's a little nervous being in a new house," Mum told the two workers.

"She *always* acts like that," I told them.

A few minutes later, the men had gone. Mum was in her room, trying to mend her sweater. And I was alone in the family room with my piano.

I sat on the bench and slid back and forth on it. The bench was polished and smooth. It was really slippery.

I planned a really funny comedy act where I sit down to play the piano for Mum and Dad, only the bench is so slippery, I keep sliding right onto the floor.

I practised sliding and falling for a while. I was having fun.

Falling is one of my hobbies. It isn't as easy as it looks.

After a while, I got tired of falling. I just sat on the bench and stared at the keys. I tried picking out a tune, hitting notes until I found the right ones.

I started to get excited about learning to play the piano.

I imagined it was going to be fun.

I was wrong. Very wrong.

On Saturday afternoon, I stood staring out of the living room window. It was a blustery, grey day. It looked as if it was about to snow.

I saw the piano teacher walking up the drive. He was right on time. Two o'clock.

154

Pressing my face against the window, I could see that he was quite a big man. He wore a long, puffy red coat and he had bushy white hair. From this distance, he sort of looked like Santa Claus.

He walked very stiffly, as if his knees weren't good. Arthritis or something, I suppose.

Dad had found his name in a tiny ad in the back of the New Goshen newspaper. He showed it to me. It said:

THE SHREEK SCHOOL
New Method Piano Training

Since it was the only ad in the paper for a piano teacher, Dad phoned the number.

And now, Mum and Dad were greeting the teacher at the door and taking his heavy red coat. "Jerry, this is Dr Shreek," Dad said, motioning for me to leave my place by the window.

Dr Shreek smiled at me. "Hello, Jerry."

He really did look like Santa Claus, except he had a white moustache and no beard. He had round, red cheeks and a friendly smile, and his blue eyes sort of twinkled as he greeted me.

He wore a white shirt that was coming un-tucked around his big belly, and baggy, grey trousers.

I stepped forward and shook hands with him. His hand was red and kind of spongy. "Nice to meet you, Dr Shreek," I said politely.

Mum and Dad grinned at each other. They could never believe it when I was polite!

Dr Shreek put his spongy hand on my shoulder. "I know I have a funny name," he said, chuckling. "I probably should change it. But, you have to admit, it's a real attention-getter!"

We all laughed.

Dr Shreek's expression turned serious. "Have you ever played an instrument before, Jerry?"

I thought hard. "Well, I had a kazoo once!"

Everyone laughed again.

"The piano is a little more difficult than the kazoo," Dr Shreek said, still chuckling. "Let me see your piano."

I led him through the dining room and into the family room. He walked stiffly, but it didn't seem to slow him down.

Mum and Dad excused themselves and disappeared upstairs to do more unpacking.

Dr Shreek studied the piano keys. Then he lifted the back and examined the strings with his eyes. "Very fine instrument," he murmured. "Very fine."

"We found it here," I told him.

His mouth opened in a little O of surprise. "You found it!"

"In the attic. Someone just left it up there," I said.

"How strange," he replied, rubbing his pudgy chin. He straightened his white moustache as he stared at the keys. "Don't you wonder who played this piano before you?" he asked softly. "Don't you wonder whose fingers touched these keys?"

"Well . . ." I really didn't know what to say.

"What a mystery," he said in a whisper. Then he motioned for me to take a seat on the piano bench.

I was tempted to do my comedy act and slide right off onto the floor. But I decided I'd save it for when I knew him better.

He seemed like a nice, jolly kind of man. But I didn't want him to think I wasn't serious about learning to play.

He dropped down beside me on the bench. He was so wide, there was barely room for the two of us.

"Will you be giving me lessons here at home every week?" I asked, scooting over as far as I could to make room.

"I'll give you lessons at home at first," he replied, his blue eyes twinkling at me. "Then, if you show promise, Jerry, you can come to my school."

I started to say something, but he grabbed my hands.

"Let me take a look," he said, raising my hands close to his face. He turned them over and studied both sides. Then he carefully examined my fingers.

"What beautiful hands!" he exclaimed breathlessly. "Excellent hands!"

I stared down at my hands. They didn't look like anything special to me. Just normal hands.

"Excellent hands," Dr Shreek repeated. He placed them carefully on the piano keys. He showed me what each note was, starting with C, and he had me play each one with the correct finger.

"Next week we will start," he told me, climbing up from the piano bench. "I just wanted to meet you today."

He searched through a small bag he had leaned against the wall. He pulled out a workbook and handed it to me. It was called *Beginning to Play: A Hands-On Approach.*

"Look this over, Jerry. Try to learn the notes on pages two and three." He made his way over to his coat, which Dad had draped over the back of the sofa.

"See you next Saturday," I said. I felt a little disappointed that the lesson had been so short. I thought I'd be playing some great rock riffs by now.

He pulled on his coat, then came back to where I was sitting. "I think you will be an excellent pupil, Jerry," he said, smiling.

I muttered thanks. I was surprised to see that his eyes had settled on my hands. "Excellent. Excellent," he whispered.

I felt a sudden chill.

I think it was the hungry expression on his face.

What's so special about my hands? I wondered. *Why does he like them so much?*

It was weird. Definitely weird.

But of course I didn't know *how* weird . . .

CDEFGABC.

I practised the notes on pages two and three of the piano workbook. The book showed which finger to use and everything.

This is easy, I thought.

So when can I start playing some rock and roll?

I was still picking out notes when Mum surfaced from the basement and poked her head into the family room. Her hair had come loose from the bandanna she had tied around her head, and she had dirty smudges on her forehead.

"Has Dr Shreek left already?" she asked, surprised.

"Yeah. He said he just wanted to meet me," I told her. "He's coming back next Saturday. He said I had excellent hands."

"Have you?" She brushed the hair out of her eyes. "Well, maybe you can take those excellent hands down to the basement and use them to help us unpack some boxes."

"Oh, no!" I cried, and I slid off the piano bench and fell to the floor.

She didn't laugh.

That night, I heard piano music.

I sat straight up in bed and listened. The music floated up from downstairs.

I climbed out of bed. The floorboards were cold under my bare feet. I was supposed to have a carpet, but Dad hadn't had time to put it down yet.

The house was silent. Through my bedroom window, I could see a gentle snow coming down, tiny, fine flakes, grey against the black sky.

"Someone is playing the piano," I said aloud, startled by the huskiness of my sleep-filled voice. "Someone is downstairs playing my piano."

Mum and Dad must hear it, I thought. Their room is at the far end of the house. But they are downstairs. They must hear it.

I crept to my bedroom door.

The same slow, sad melody. I had been humming it just before dinner. Mum had asked me where I'd heard it, and I couldn't remember.

I leaned against the doorframe, my heart pounding, and listened. The music drifted up so clearly, I could hear each note.

161

Who is playing?

Who?

I had to find out. Trailing my hand along the wall, I hurried through the dark passage. There was a night-light by the stairway, but I was always forgetting to turn it on.

I made my way to the stairs. Then, gripping the wooden banister tightly, I crept down, one step at a time, trying to be silent.

Trying not to scare the piano player away.

The wooden stairs creaked quietly under my weight. But the music continued. Soft and sad, almost mournful.

Tiptoeing and holding my breath, I crossed the living room. A streetlight cast a wash of pale yellow across the floor. Through the large front window, I could see the tiny snowflakes drifting down.

I nearly tripped over an unpacked case of vases left next to the coffee table. But I grabbed the back of the sofa and kept myself from falling.

The music stopped. Then started again.

I leaned against the sofa, waiting for my heart to stop pounding so hard.

Where are Mum and Dad? I wondered, staring towards the back hallway where their room was.

Can't they hear the piano, too? Aren't they curious? Don't they wonder who is in the family room in the middle of the night, playing such a sad song?

162

I took a deep breath and pushed myself away from the sofa. Slowly, silently, I made my way through the dining room.

It was darker back there. No light from the street. I moved carefully, aware of all the chairs and table legs that could trip me up.

The door to the family room stood just a few feet ahead of me. The music grew louder.

I took a step. Then another.

I moved into the open doorway.

Who is it? Who is it?

I peered into the darkness.

But before I could see anything, someone uttered a horrifying shriek behind me—and shoved me hard, pushing me down to the floor.

163

I hit the floor hard on my knees and elbows.

Another loud shriek—right in my ears.

My shoulders throbbed with pain.

The light came on.

"Bonkers!" I roared.

The cat leapt off my shoulders and scurried out of the room.

"Jerry—what are you doing? What's going on?" Mum demanded angrily as she ran into the room.

"What's all the racket?" Dad was right behind her, squinting hard without his glasses.

"Bonkers jumped on me!" I screamed, still on the floor. "Ow. My shoulder. That stupid cat!"

"But, Jerry—" Mum started. She bent to help pull me up.

"That stupid cat!" I fumed. "She jumped down from that shelf. She scared me to death. And look—look at my pyjama top!"

The cat's claws had ripped right through the shoulder.

"Are you cut? Are you bleeding?" Mum asked, pulling the shirt collar down to examine my shoulder.

"We really have to do something about that cat," Dad muttered. "Jerry is right. She's a menace."

Mum immediately jumped to Bonkers' defence. "She was just frightened, that's all. She probably thought Jerry was a burglar."

"A burglar?" I shrieked in a voice so high, only dogs could hear me. "How could she think I was a burglar? Aren't cats supposed to see in the dark?"

"Well, what were you doing down here, Jerry?" Mum asked, straightening my pyjama top collar. She patted my shoulder. As if that would help.

"Yeah. Why were you skulking around down here?" Dad demanded, squinting hard at me. He could barely see a thing without his glasses.

"I wasn't skulking around," I replied angrily. "I heard piano music and—"

"You *what*?" Mum interrupted.

"I heard piano music. In the family room. So I came down to see who was playing."

My parents were both staring at me as if I were a Martian.

"Didn't you hear it?" I cried.

They shook their heads.

I turned to the piano. No one there. Of course.

I hurried over to the piano bench, leaned down, and rubbed my hand over the surface.

It was warm.

"Someone was sitting here. I can tell!" I exclaimed.

"Not funny," Mum said, making a face.

"Not funny, Jerry," Dad echoed. "You came down here to pull some kind of prank—didn't you!" he accused.

"Huh? Me?"

"Don't play the innocent, Jerome," Mum said, rolling her eyes. "We know you. You're *never* innocent."

"I wasn't joking!" I cried angrily. "I heard music, someone playing—"

"Who?" Dad demanded. "Who was playing?"

"Maybe it was Bonkers," Mum laughed.

Dad laughed too, but I didn't.

"What was the joke, Jerry? What were you planning to do?" Dad asked.

"Were you going to do something to the piano?" Mum demanded, staring at me so hard, I could practically *feel* it. "That's a valuable instrument, you know."

I sighed wearily. I felt so frustrated, I wanted to shout, scream, throw a fit, and maybe slug them both. "The piano is *haunted!*" I shouted.

The words just popped into my head.

"Huh?" It was Dad's turn to give me a hard stare.

"It must be haunted!" I insisted, my voice shaking. "It keeps playing—but there's no one playing it!"

"I've heard enough," Mum muttered, shaking her head. "I'm going back to bed."

"Ghosts, huh?" Dad asked, rubbing his chin thoughtfully. He stepped up to me and lowered his head, the way he does when he's about to unload something serious. "Listen, Jerry, I know this house might seem old and kind of scary. And I know how hard it was for you to leave your friends behind and move away."

"Dad, please—" I interrupted.

But he kept going. "The house is just old, Jerry. Old and a little rundown. That doesn't mean it's haunted. These ghosts of yours—don't you see?—they're really your fears coming out."

Dad has a psychology degree.

"Skip the lecture, Dad," I told him. "I'm going to bed."

"Okay, Jer," he said, patting my shoulder. "Remember—in a few weeks, you'll know I'm right. In a few weeks, this ghost business will all seem silly to you."

167

Boy, was he wrong!

I slammed my locker shut and started to put on my jacket. The long school corridors echoed with laughing voices, slamming lockers, calls and shouts.

The corridors were always noisier on Friday afternoons. School was over, and the weekend was here!

"Oooh, what's that smell?" I cried, making a disgusted face.

Beside me, a girl was down on her knees, pawing through a pile of junk on the floor of her locker. "I *wondered* where that apple disappeared to!" she exclaimed.

She climbed to her feet, holding a shrivelled, brown apple in one hand. The sour odour invaded my nostrils. I thought I was going to throw up!

I must have been making a funny face, because she burst out laughing. "Hungry?" She pushed the disgusting thing in my face.

"No thanks." I pushed it back towards her. "You can have it."

She laughed again. She was quite pretty. She had long, straight black hair and green eyes.

She put the rotten apple down on the floor. "You're the new kid, right?" she asked. "I'm Kim. Kim Li Chin."

"Hi," I said. I told her my name. "You're in my maths class. And science class," I told her.

She turned back to her locker, searching for more stuff. "I know," she replied. "I saw you fall out of your chair when Miss Klein asked you a question."

"I just did that to be funny," I explained quickly. "I didn't really fall."

"I know," she said. She pulled a heavy grey wool sweater down over her lighter sweater. Then she reached down and removed a black violin case from her locker.

"Is that your lunchbox?" I joked.

"I'm late for my violin lesson," she answered, slamming her locker shut. She struggled to push the padlock closed.

"I'm taking piano lessons," I told her. "Well, I mean I've just started."

"You know, I live opposite you," she said, adjusting her rucksack over her shoulder. "I watched you move in."

"Really?" I replied, surprised. "Well, maybe you could come over and we could play together. I mean, play music. You know. I'm taking lessons every Saturday with Dr Shreek."

Her mouth dropped open in horror as she stared at me. "You're doing *what?*" she cried.

"Taking piano lessons with Dr Shreek," I repeated.

"Oh!" She uttered a soft cry, spun round, and began running towards the front door.

"Hey, Kim—" I called after her. "Kim—what's wrong?"

But she had disappeared out of the door.

"Excellent hands. Excellent!" Dr Shreek declared.

"Thanks," I replied awkwardly.

I was seated at the piano bench, hunched over the piano, my hands spread over the keys. Dr Shreek stood beside me, staring down at my hands.

"Now play the piece again," he instructed, raising his blue eyes to mine. His smile faded beneath his white moustache as his expression turned serious. "Play it carefully, my boy. Slowly and carefully. Concentrate on your fingers. Each finger is alive, remember—*alive!*"

"My fingers are alive," I repeated, staring down at them.

What a weird thought, I told myself.

I began to play, concentrating on the notes on the music sheet propped above the keyboard. It was a simple melody, a beginner's piece by Bach.

I thought it sounded pretty good.

"The fingers! The fingers!" Dr Shreek cried. He leaned down towards the keyboard, bringing his face close to mine. "Remember, the fingers are alive!"

What's with this guy and fingers? I asked myself.

I finished the piece. I glanced up to see a frown darken his face.

"Pretty good, Jerry," he said softly. "Now let us try it a bit faster."

"I goofed up the middle bit," I confessed.

"You lost your concentration," he replied. He reached down and spread my fingers over the keys. "Again," he instructed. "But faster. And concentrate. Concentrate on your hands."

I took a deep breath and began the piece again. But this time I messed it up immediately.

I started again. It sounded pretty good. Only a few dud notes.

I wondered if Mum and Dad could hear it. Then I remembered they had gone grocery shopping.

Dr Shreek and I were alone in the house.

I finished the piece and lowered my hands to my lap with a sigh.

"Not bad. Now faster," Dr Shreek ordered.

"Maybe we should try another piece," I suggested. "This is getting pretty boring."

"Faster this time," he replied, totally ignoring

me. "The hands, Jerry. Remember the hands. They're alive. Let them breathe!"

Let them breathe?

I stared down at my hands, expecting them to talk back to me!

"Begin," Dr Shreek instructed sternly, leaning over me. "Faster."

Sighing, I began to play again. The same boring tune.

"Faster!" the instructor cried. "Faster, Jerry!"

I played faster. My fingers moved over the keys, pounding them hard. I tried to concentrate on the notes, but I was playing too fast for my eyes to keep up.

"Faster!" Dr Shreek cried excitedly, staring down at the keys. "That's it! Faster, Jerry!"

My fingers were moving so fast, they were a blur!

"Faster! Faster!"

Was I playing the right notes? I couldn't tell. It was too fast, too fast to *hear*!

"Faster, Jerry!" Dr Shreek instructed, screaming at the top of his lungs. "Faster! The hands are alive! Alive!"

"I can't do it!" I cried. "Please—!"

"Faster! Faster!"

"I can't!" I insisted. It was too fast. Too fast to play. Too fast to hear.

I tried to stop.

But my hands kept going!

"Stop! Stop!" I screamed down at them in horror.

"Faster! Play faster!" Dr Shreek ordered, his eyes wide with excitement, his face bright red. "The hands are *alive!*"

"No—please! Stop!" I called down to my hands. "Stop playing!"

But they really *were* alive. They wouldn't stop.

My fingers flew over the keys. A crazy tidal wave of notes flooded the family room.

"Faster! Faster!" the instructor ordered.

And despite my frightened cries to stop, my hands gleefully obeyed him, playing on, faster and faster and faster.

Faster and faster, the music swirled around me.

It's choking me, I thought, gasping for breath. I can't breathe.

I struggled to stop my hands. But they moved frantically over the keys, playing louder. Louder.

My hands began to ache. They throbbed with pain.

But still they played. Faster. Louder.

Until I woke up.

I sat up in bed, wide awake.

And realized I was sitting on my hands.

They both tingled painfully. Pins and needles. My hands had fallen asleep.

I had been asleep. The weird piano lesson—it was a dream.

A strange nightmare.

"It's still Friday night," I said aloud. The sound of my voice helped bring me out of the dream.

175

I shook my hands, trying to get the circulation going, trying to stop the uncomfortable tingling.

My forehead was sweating, a cold sweat. My whole body felt clammy. The pyjama top stuck damply to my back. I shuddered, suddenly chilled.

And realized the piano music hadn't stopped.

I gasped and gripped the bedcovers tightly. Holding my breath, I listened.

The notes floated into my dark bedroom.

Not the frantic roar of notes from my dream. The slow, sad melody I had heard before.

Still trembling from my frightening dream, I climbed silently out of bed.

The music floated up from the family room, so soft, so mournful.

Who is playing down there?

My hands still tingled as I made my way over the cold floorboards to the doorway. I stopped in the hall and listened.

The tune ended, then began again.

Tonight I am going to solve this mystery, I told myself.

My heart was pounding. My whole body was tingling now. Pins and needles up and down my back.

Ignoring how frightened I felt, I walked quietly down the hall to the staircase. The dim night-light down near the floor made my shadow rise up on the wall.

176

It startled me for a moment. I hung back. But then I hurried down the stairs, leaning hard on the banister to keep the steps from creaking.

The piano music grew louder as I crossed the dark living room.

Nothing is going to stop me tonight, I told myself. Nothing.

Tonight I am going to see who is playing the piano.

The music continued, soft high notes, so light and sad.

I tiptoed carefully through the living room, holding my breath, listening to the music.

I stepped up to the doorway to the family room.

The music continued, a little louder.

The same melody, over and over again.

Peering into the darkness, I stepped into the room.

One step. Another.

The piano was only a few feet in front of me.

The music was so clear, so close.

But I couldn't see anyone on the piano bench. I couldn't see anyone there at all.

Who is playing? Who is playing this sad, sad music in the darkness?

Trembling all over, I took another step closer. Another step.

"Who—who's there!" I called out in a choked whisper.

I stopped, my hands knotted tensely into tight fists at my sides. I stared hard into the blackness, straining to see.

The music continued. I could hear fingers on the keys, hear the slide of feet on the pedals.

"Who's there? Who's playing?" My voice was tiny and shrill.

There's *no one* here, I realized to my horror. The piano is playing, but there's *no one* here.

Then, slowly, very slowly, like a grey cloud forming in the night sky, the ghost began to appear.

At first I could just see faint outlines, pale lines of grey moving against the blackness.

I gasped. My heart was pounding so hard, I thought it would burst.

The grey lines took shape, began to fill in.

I stood frozen in terror, too frightened to run or even look away.

And as I stared, a woman came into view. I couldn't tell if she was young or old. She had her head down and her eyes closed, and was concentrating on the piano keys.

She had long, wavy hair hanging loose down to her shoulders. She wore a short-sleeved top and a long skirt. Her face, her skin, her hair—all grey. Everything was grey.

She continued to play as if I weren't standing there.

Her eyes were closed. Her lips formed a sad smile.

She was quite pretty, I realized.

But she was a ghost. A ghost playing the piano in our family room.

"Who are you? What are you doing here?" My high-pitched, tight voice startled me. The words came flying out, almost beyond my control.

She stopped playing and opened her eyes. She stared hard at me, studying me. Her smile faded quickly. Her face revealed no emotion at all.

I stared back, into the grey. It was like looking at someone in a heavy, dark fog.

With the music stopped, the house had become so quiet, so terrifyingly quiet. "Who—who are you?" I repeated, stammering in my tiny voice.

Her grey eyes narrowed in sadness. "This is my house," she said. Her voice was a dry whisper, as dry as dead leaves. As dry as death.

"This is my house." The whispered words seemed to come from far away, so soft I wasn't sure I had heard them.

"I—don't understand," I choked out, feeling a cold chill at the back of my neck. "What are you doing here?"

"My house," came the whispered reply. "My piano."

"But who *are* you?" I repeated. "Are you a *ghost?*"

As I uttered my frightened question, she let out

a loud sigh. And as I stared into the greyness, I saw her face begin to change.

The eyes closed, and her cheeks began to droop. Her grey skin appeared to fall, to melt away. It drooped like biscuit batter, like soft clay. It fell onto her shoulders, then tumbled to the floor. Her hair followed, falling off in thick clumps.

A silent cry escaped my lips as her skull was revealed. Her grey skull.

Nothing remained of her face except for her eyes, her grey eyes, which bulged in the open sockets, staring at me through the darkness.

"Stay away from my piano!" she rasped. *"I'm warning you—STAY AWAY!"*

I backed up and turned away from the hideous, rasping skull. I tried to scramble away, but my legs didn't cooperate.

I fell.

Hit the floor on my knees.

I struggled to pull myself up, but I was shaking too hard.

"Stay away from my piano!" The grey skull glared at me with its bulging eyes.

"Mum! Dad!" I tried to scream, but it came out a muffled whisper.

I scrambled to my feet, my heart pounding, my throat closed tight with fear.

"This is my house! My piano! STAY AWAY!"

"Mum! Help me! Dad!"

This time I managed to call out. "Mum—Dad —please!"

To my relief, I heard bumping and clattering in the hall. Heavy footsteps.

"Jerry? Jerry? Where are you?" Mum called. "Ow!" I heard her bump into something in the dining room.

Dad reached the family room first.

I grabbed him by the shoulders, then pointed. "Dad—look! A ghost! It's a GHOST!"

182

Dad clicked on the light. Mum stumbled into the room, holding one knee.

I pointed in horror to the piano bench.

Which was now empty.

"The ghost—I saw her!" I cried, shaking all over. I turned to my parents. "Did you hear her? *Did* you?"

"Jerry, calm down." Dad put his hands on my trembling shoulders. "Calm down. It's okay. Everything is okay."

"But did you see her?" I demanded. "She was sitting there, playing the piano, and—"

"Ow. I really hurt my knee," Mum groaned. "I bumped it on the coffee table. Oww."

"Her skin dropped off. Her eyes bulged out of her skull!" I told them. I couldn't get that grinning skull out of my mind. I could still see her, as if her picture had been burned into my eyes.

"There's no one there," Dad said softly,

183

holding onto my shoulders. "See? No one."

"Did you have a nightmare?" Mum asked, bending to massage her knee.

"It *wasn't* a nightmare!" I screamed. "I *saw* her! I really did! She *talked* to me. She told me this was her piano, her house."

"Let's sit down and talk about this," Mum suggested. "Would you like a cup of hot cocoa?"

"You don't believe me—*do* you?" I cried angrily. "I'm telling you the *truth!*"

"We don't really believe in ghosts," Dad said quietly. He guided me to the red leather sofa against the wall and sat down beside me. Yawning, Mum followed us, lowering herself onto the sofa arm.

"You don't believe in ghosts, do you, Jerry?" Mum asked.

"I do now!" I exclaimed. "Why don't you listen to me? I *heard* her playing the piano. I came downstairs and I saw her. She was a woman. She was all grey. And her face fell off. And her skull showed through. And—and—"

I saw Mum give Dad a look.

Why wouldn't they believe me?

"A woman at work was telling me about a doctor," Mum said softly, reaching down and taking my hand. "A nice doctor who talks to young people. Dr Frye, I think his name was."

"Huh? You mean a psychiatrist?" I cried

shrilly. "You think I'm *crazy?*"

"No, of course not," Mum replied quickly, still holding on to my hand. "I think something has made you very nervous, Jerry. And I don't think it would hurt to talk to someone about it."

"What are you nervous about, Jer?" Dad asked, straightening the collar of his pyjama top. "Is it the new house? Going to a new school?"

"Is it the piano lessons?" Mum asked. "Are you worried about the lessons?" She glanced at the piano, gleaming black and shiny under the ceiling light.

"No. I'm not worried about the lessons," I muttered unhappily. "I *told* you—I'm worried about the *ghost!*"

"I'm going to make you an appointment with Dr Frye," Mum said quietly. "Tell him about the ghost, Jerry. I bet he can explain it all better than your father and I can."

"I'm not mad," I muttered.

"Something has upset you. Something is giving you bad dreams," Dad said. "This doctor will be able to explain it to you." He yawned and stood up, stretching his arms above his head. "I've got to get some sleep."

"Me, too," Mum said, letting go of my hand and climbing off the arm of the sofa. "Do you think you can go to sleep now, Jerry?"

I shook my head and muttered, "I don't know."

"Do you want us to walk you to your room?" she asked.

"I'm not a little baby!" I shouted. I felt angry and frustrated. I wanted to scream and scream until they believed me.

"Well, good night, Jer," Dad said. "Tomorrow's Saturday, so you can sleep late."

"Yeah. Right," I muttered.

"If you have any more bad dreams, wake us up," Mum said.

Dad clicked off the light. They headed down the hall to their room.

I made my way across the living room to the front stairs.

I was so angry, I wanted to hit something or kick something. I was really insulted, too.

But as I climbed the creaking stairs in the darkness, my anger turned to fear.

The ghost had vanished from the family room. What if she was waiting for me up in my room?

What if I walked into my room and the disgusting grey skull with the bulging eyeballs was staring at me from my bed?

The floorboards squeaked and groaned beneath me as I slowly made my way along the passage to my room. I suddenly felt cold all over. My throat tightened. I struggled to breathe.

186

She's in there. She's in there waiting for me.

I knew it. I knew she'd be there.

And if I scream, if I cry for help, Mum and Dad will just think I'm crazy.

What does the ghost want?

Why does she play the piano every night? Why did she try to frighten me? Why did she tell me to stay away?

The questions rolled through my mind. I couldn't answer them. I was too tired, too frightened to think clearly.

I hesitated outside my room, breathing hard.

Then, holding onto the wall, I gathered my courage and stepped inside.

As I moved into the darkness, the ghost rose up in front of my bed.

I uttered a choked cry and staggered back to the doorway.

Then I realized I was staring at my covers. I must have kicked them over the foot of the bed during my nightmare about Dr Shreek. They were lying in a heap on the floor.

My heart pounding, I crept back into the room, grabbed the blanket and sheet, and pulled them back onto the bed.

Maybe I *am* cracking up! I thought.

No way, I assured myself. I might be scared and frustrated and angry—but I saw what I saw.

Shivering, I slid into bed and pulled the covers up to my chin. I closed my eyes and tried to force the picture of the ugly grey skull from my mind.

When I finally started to drift off to sleep, I heard the piano music start again.

Dr Shreek arrived promptly at two the next afternoon. Mum and Dad were out in the garage, unpacking more boxes. I took Dr Shreek's coat, then led him into the family room.

It was a cold, blustery day outside, threatening snow. Dr Shreek's cheeks were pink from the cold. With his white hair and moustache, and round belly under his baggy, white shirt, he looked more like Santa Claus than ever.

He rubbed his pudgy hands together to warm them and motioned for me to take a seat at the piano bench. "Such a beautiful instrument," he said cheerily, running a hand over the shiny, black top of the piano. "You are a very lucky young man to find this waiting for you."

"I suppose so," I replied without enthusiasm.

I had slept till eleven, but I was still tired. And I couldn't shake the ghost and her warning from my mind.

"Have you practised your chords?" Dr Shreek asked, leaning against the piano, turning the pages of the music workbook.

"A little," I told him.

"Let me see what you have learned. Here." He began to place my fingers over the keys. "Remember? This is where you start."

I played a scale.

"Excellent hands," Dr Shreek said, smiling. "Keep repeating it, please."

The lesson went well. He kept telling me how good I was, even though I was just playing notes and a simple scale.

Maybe I *do* have some talent, I thought.

I asked him when I could begin learning some rock riffs.

He chuckled for some reason. "In due course," he replied, staring at my hands.

I heard Mum and Dad come in through the kitchen door. A few seconds later, Mum appeared in the living room, rubbing the arms of her sweater. "It's really getting cold out there," she said, smiling at Dr Shreek. "I think it's going to snow."

"It's nice and warm in here," he replied, returning her smile.

"How's the lesson going?" Mum asked him.

"Very well," Dr Shreek told her, winking at me. "I think Jerry shows a lot of promise. I would like him to start taking his lessons at my school."

"That's wonderful!" Mum exclaimed. "Do you really think he has talent?"

"He has excellent hands," Dr Shreek replied.

Something about the way he said it gave me a cold chill.

"Do you teach rock music at your school?" I asked.

He patted my shoulder. "We teach all kinds of

music. My school is very large, and we have many fine instructors. We have pupils of all ages there. Do you think you could come after school on Fridays?"

"That would be fine," Mum said.

Dr Shreek crossed the room and handed my mum a card. "Here is the address of my school. I'm afraid it is at the other end of town."

"No problem," Mum said, studying the card. "I get off work early on Fridays. I can drive him."

"That will end our lesson for today, Jerry," Dr Shreek said. "Practise the new chords. And I'll see you on Friday."

He followed my mum to the living room. I heard them chatting quietly, but I couldn't make out what they were saying.

I stood up and walked to the window. It had started to snow, very large flakes coming down really hard. The snow was already starting to stick.

Staring into the back garden, I wondered if there were any good hills to go sledging on in New Goshen. And I wondered if my sledge had been unpacked.

I cried out when the piano suddenly started to play.

Loud, jangling noise. Like someone pounding furiously on the keys with heavy fists.

Pound. Pound. Pound.

"Jerry—stop it!" Mum shouted from the living room.

"I'm not doing it!" I cried.

192

Dr Frye's office wasn't the way I imagined a psychiatrist's office. It was small and bright. The walls were yellow, and there were colourful pictures of parrots and toucans and other birds hanging all around.

He didn't have a black leather couch like psychiatrists always have on TV and in films. Instead, he had two soft-looking, green armchairs. He didn't even have a desk. Just the two chairs.

I sat in one, and he sat in the other.

He was a lot younger than I thought he'd be. He looked younger than my dad. He had wavy red hair, slicked down with some kind of gel or something, I think. And he had a face full of freckles.

He just didn't look like a psychiatrist at all.

"Tell me about your new house," he said. He had his legs crossed. He rested his long notepad on them as he studied me.

"It's a big, old house," I told him. "That's about it."

He asked me to describe my room, so I did.

Then we talked about the house we'd moved from and my old room. Then we talked about my friends at my old home. Then we talked about my new school.

I felt nervous at first. But he seemed okay. He listened carefully to everything I said. And he didn't give me funny looks, as if I was crazy or something.

Even when I told him about the ghost.

He scribbled down a few notes when I told him about the piano playing late at night. He stopped writing when I told him how I'd seen the ghost, and how her hair fell off and then her face, and how she had screamed at me to stay away.

"My parents didn't believe me," I said, squeezing the soft arms of the chair. My hands were sweating.

"It's a pretty weird story," Dr Frye replied. "If you were your mum and dad, and your kid told you that story, would *you* believe it?"

"Of course," I said. "If it was true."

He chewed on his pencil rubber and stared at me.

"Do you think I'm crazy?" I asked.

He lowered his notepad. He didn't smile at the question. "No. I don't think you're crazy, Jerry. But the human mind can be really strange sometimes."

Then he launched into this long lecture about how sometimes we're afraid of something, but we don't admit to ourselves that we're afraid. So our mind does all kinds of things to show that we're afraid, even though we keep telling ourselves that we're *not* afraid.

In other words, he didn't believe me, either.

"Moving to a new house creates all kinds of stress," he said. "It is possible to start imagining that we see things, that we hear things—just so we don't admit to ourselves what we're *really* afraid of."

"I didn't imagine the piano music," I said. "I can hum the melody for you. And I didn't imagine the ghost. I can tell you just what she looked like."

"Let's talk about it next week," he said, getting to his feet. "Our time is up. But until next time, I just want to assure you that your mind is perfectly normal. You're not crazy, Jerry. You shouldn't think that for a second."

He shook my hand. "You'll see," he said, opening the door for me. "You'll be amazed at what we work out is behind that ghost of yours."

I muttered thanks and walked out of his office.

I made my way through the empty waiting room and stepped into the hallway.

And then I felt the ghost's icy grip tighten around my neck.

196

The unearthly cold shot through my whole body.

Uttering a terrified cry, I jerked away and spun round to face her.

"Mum!" I cried, my voice shrill and tiny.

"Sorry my hands are so cold," she replied calmly, unaware of how badly she had scared me. "It's *freezing* out. Didn't you hear me calling you?"

"No," I told her. My neck still tingled. I tried to rub the cold away. "I . . . uh . . . was thinking about something, and—"

"Well, I didn't mean to scare you," she said, leading the way across the small car park to the car. She stopped to pull the car keys from her bag. "Did you and Dr Frye have a nice talk?"

"Sort of," I said.

This ghost has me jumping out of my skin, I realized as I climbed into the car. Now I'm seeing the ghost *everywhere.*

197

I have *got* to calm down, I told myself. I've just *got* to.

I've got to stop thinking that the ghost is following me.

But how?

Friday after school, Mum drove me to Dr Shreek's music school. It was a cold, grey day. I stared at my breath steaming up the passenger window as we drove. It had snowed the day before, and the roads were still icy, and slick.

"I hope we're not late," Mum fretted. We stopped for a light. She cleared the windscreen in front of her with the back of her gloved hand. "I'm afraid to drive any faster than this."

All of the cars were inching along. We drove past a crowd of kids building a snow fort in a front garden. One red-faced little kid was crying because the others wouldn't let him join them.

"The school is practically in the next town," Mum remarked, pumping the brakes as we slid towards a junction. "I wonder why Dr Shreek has his school so far away from everything."

"I don't know," I answered dully. I was quite nervous. "Do you think Dr Shreek will be my instructor? Or do you think I'll have someone else?"

Mum shrugged her shoulders. She leaned forward over the steering wheel, struggling to see through the steamed-up windscreen.

Finally, we turned onto the street where the school was located. I stared out at the street of dark, old houses. The houses gave way to woods, the bare trees tilting up under a white blanket of snow.

On the other side of the woods stood a brick building, half-hidden behind tall hedges. "This must be the school," Mum said, stopping the car in the middle of the street and staring up at the old building. "There's no sign or anything. But it's the only building for streets."

"It's creepy-looking," I said.

Squinting through the windscreen, she pulled the car into the narrow gravel drive, nearly hidden by the tall, snow-covered hedges.

"Are you sure this is it?" I asked. I cleared a spot on the window with my hand and peered through it. The old building looked more like a prison than a school. It had rows of tiny windows above the ground floor, and the windows were all barred. Thick ivy covered the front of the building, making it appear even darker than it was.

"I'm fairly sure," Mum said, biting her lip. She lowered the window and stuck her head out, gazing up at the enormous, old house.

The sound of piano music floated into the car. Notes and scales and melodies all mixed together.

"Yeah. We've found it!" Mum declared happily. "Go on, Jerry. Hurry. You're late. I'm going to go and pick up something for dinner. I'll be back in an hour."

I pushed open the car door and stepped out onto the snowy drive. My boots crunched loudly as I started to jog towards the building.

The piano music grew louder. Scales and songs jumbled together into a deafening rumble of noise.

A narrow walk led up to the front entrance. The walk hadn't been shovelled, and a layer of ice had formed under the snow. I slipped and nearly fell as I approached the entrance.

I stopped and gazed up. It looks more like a haunted house than a music school, I thought with a shiver.

Why did I have such a heavy feeling of dread?

Just nervous, I told myself.

Shrugging away my feeling, I turned the cold brass doorknob and pushed the heavy door. It creaked open slowly. Taking a deep breath, I stepped into the school.

A long, narrow corridor stretched before me. The corridor was surprisingly dark. Coming in from the bright, white snow, it took my eyes a long time to adjust.

The walls were a dark tile. My boots thudded noisily on the hard floor. Piano notes echoed through the corridor. The music seemed to burst out from all directions.

Where is Dr Shreek's office? I wondered.

I made my way down the corridor. The lights grew dimmer. I turned into another long corridor, and the piano music grew louder.

There were dark brown doors on both sides of this corridor. The doors had small, round windows in them. As I continued walking, I glanced into the windows.

I could see smiling instructors in each room, their heads bobbing in rhythm to piano music.

Searching for the office, I passed door after door. Each room had a pupil and an instructor inside. The piano sounds became a roar, like an ocean of music crashing against the dark tiled walls.

Dr Shreek really has a lot of pupils, I thought. There must be a hundred pianos playing at once!

I turned another corner and then another.

I suddenly realized I had completely lost my sense of direction. I had no idea where I was. I couldn't find my way back to the front door if I wanted to!

"Dr Shreek, where are you?" I muttered to myself. My voice was drowned out by the booming piano music that echoed off the walls and low ceiling.

I began to feel a little frightened.

What if these dark walls twisted on forever? I imagined myself walking and walking for the rest of my life, unable to find my way out, deafened by the pounding piano music.

"Jerry, stop scaring yourself," I said aloud.

Something caught my eye. I stopped walking and stared up at the ceiling. A small, black camera was perched above my head.

It appeared to be a video camera, like the security cameras you see in banks and shops.

Was someone watching me on a TV screen somewhere?

If they were, why didn't they come and help me find the way to Dr Shreek?

I began to get angry. What kind of school *was*

this? No signs. No office. No one to greet people.

As I turned another corner, I heard a strange thumping sound. At first I thought it was just another piano in one of the practice rooms.

The thumping grew louder, closer. I stopped in the middle of the corridor and listened. A high-pitched whine rose up over the thumping sounds.

Louder. Louder.

The floor seemed to shake.

And as I stared down the corridor, an enormous monster turned the corner. Its huge, square body glowed in the dim light as if it were made of metal. Its rectangular head bobbed near the ceiling.

Its feet crashed against the hard floor as it moved to attack me. Eyes on the sides of its head flashed an angry red.

"No!" I cried, swallowing hard.

It uttered its high-pitched whine in reply. Then it lowered its gleaming head as if preparing for battle.

I spun away, determined to escape.

To my shock, as I turned, I saw Dr Shreek.

He stood just a few metres down the hall. Dr Shreek was watching the enormous creature move in on me, a pleased grin on his face.

I stopped short with a loud gasp.

Behind me, the creature was stomping closer, blasting out its angry whine.

Ahead of me, Dr Shreek, his blue eyes glowing with pleasure, blocked my escape.

I cried out, preparing to be caught from behind by the silvery monster.

But it stopped.

Silence.

No crashing of its heavy metallic feet. No shrill whine.

"Hello, Jerry," Dr Shreek said calmly, still grinning. "What are you doing all the way back here?"

Breathing hard, I pointed to the monster, which stood silently, staring down at me. "I—I—"

"You are admiring our floor sweeper?" Dr Shreek asked.

"Your *what?*" I managed to choke out.

"Our floor sweeper. It *is* rather special," Dr Shreek said. He stepped past me and put a hand on the front of the thing.

"It—it's a machine?" I stammered.

He laughed. "You didn't think it was alive, did you?"

I just gaped at it. I was still too freaked out to speak.

"Mr Toggle, our caretaker, built this for us," Dr Shreek said, rubbing his hand along the square metal front of it. "It works like a dream. Mr Toggle can build anything. He's a genius, a true genius."

"Wh-why does it have a face?" I asked, hanging back against the wall. "Why does it have eyes that light up?"

"Just Mr Toggle's sense of humour," Dr Shreek replied, chuckling. "He put in those cameras, too." He pointed to the video camera perched on the ceiling. "Mr Toggle is a mechanical genius. We couldn't do a thing without him. We really couldn't."

I took a few reluctant steps forward and admired the floor sweeper from closer up. "I—I couldn't find your office," I told Dr Shreek. "I was wandering and wandering—"

"I apologize," he replied quickly. "Let us begin your lesson. Come."

I followed him as he led the way back in the direction I had come. He walked stiffly but

205

rapidly. His white shirt was untucked in front of his big stomach. He swung his hands stiffly as he walked.

I felt really stupid. Imagine letting myself be terrified by a floor sweeper!

He pushed open one of the brown doors with a round window, and I followed him into the room. I glanced quickly around. It was a small, square room lighted by two rows of fluorescent lights on the ceiling. There was no window.

The only furniture was a small, brown upright piano, a narrow piano bench, and a music stand.

Dr Shreek motioned for me to sit down on the piano bench, and we began our lesson. He stood behind me, placing my fingers carefully on the keys, even though I now knew how to do it myself.

We practised different notes. I hit C's and D's. Then we tried E's and F's. He showed me my first chord. Then he made me do scales over and over again.

"Excellent!" he declared near the end of the hour. "Excellent work, Jerry. I'm most pleased!" His Santa Claus cheeks were bright pink beneath his white moustache.

I squeezed my hands together, trying to get rid of a cramp. "Are you going to be my teacher?" I asked.

He nodded. "Yes, I will instruct you in the

basics," he replied. "Then when your hands are ready, you will be given over to one of our fine teachers."

When my hands are ready?

What exactly did he mean by that?

"Let us try this short piece," he said, reaching over me to turn the page in the music book. "Now, this piece has only three notes. But you must pay attention to the quarter notes and the half notes. Do you remember how long to hold a half note?"

I demonstrated on the piano. Then I tried to play the short melody. I did pretty well. Only a few naff notes.

"Wonderful! Wonderful!" Dr Shreek declared, staring at my hands as I played. He glanced at his watch. "I'm afraid our time is up. See you next Friday, Jerry. Be sure to practise what I've showed you."

I thanked him and climbed to my feet. I was glad the lesson was over. Having to concentrate so hard was really tiring. Both my hands were sweating, and I still had a cramp in one.

I headed for the door, then stopped. "Which way do I go?" I asked. "How do I get to the front?"

Dr Shreek was busy collecting the work sheets we had used, tucking them into the music book. "Just keep going left," he said without looking up. "You can't miss it."

I said goodbye and stepped out into the dark hallway. My ears were immediately attacked by the roar of the piano notes.

Aren't the other lessons over? I wondered.

How come they keep playing them even though the hour is up?

I glanced in both directions, making sure there were no floor sweepers waiting to attack. Then I turned left, as Dr Shreek had instructed, and began to follow the corridor towards the front.

As I passed door after door, I could see the smiling instructors inside each room, their heads moving in rhythm with the piano playing.

Most of the pupils in these rooms were more advanced than me, I realized. They weren't practising notes and scales. They were playing long, complicated pieces.

I turned left, then when the corridor came to an end, turned left one more time.

It took me a while to realize that I was lost again.

Had I missed a left turn somewhere?

The dark halls with their rows of brown doors on both sides all looked alike.

I turned left again. My heart began to pound. Why wasn't anyone else in the hall?

Then up ahead I saw double doors. The front exit must be through those doors, I decided.

I made my way eagerly to the double doors and started to push through them—when powerful hands grabbed me from behind, and a gruff voice rasped in my ear, "No, you don't!"

"Huh?" I uttered a silent cry.

The hands pulled me back, then let go of my shoulders.

The double doors swung back into place.

I spun round to see a tall, wiry man with long, scraggly black hair and a stubbly black beard. He wore a yellow T-shirt under denim dungarees.

"Not that way," he said softly. "You're looking for the front? It's up there." He pointed to the hall to the left.

"Oh. Sorry," I said, breathing hard. "You . . . scared me."

The man apologized. "I'll take you to the front," he offered, scratching his stubbly cheek. "Allow me to introduce myself. I'm Mr Toggle."

"Oh. Hi," I said. "I'm Jerry Hawkins. Dr Shreek told me about you. I—I saw your floor sweeper."

He smiled. His black eyes lit up like dark coals. "It's a beauty, isn't it? I have a few other creations like it, some even better."

"Dr Shreek says you're a mechanical genius," I gushed.

Mr Toggle chuckled to himself. "Yes. I programmed him to say that!" he joked. We both laughed.

"Next time you come to the school, I'll show you some of my other inventions," Mr Toggle offered, adjusting his dungaree straps over his slender shoulders.

"Thanks," I replied. The front door was right up ahead. I was never so glad to see a door! "I'm sure I'll catch on to the layout of this place," I said.

He didn't seem to hear me. "Dr Shreek tells me you have excellent hands," he said, a strange smile forming under his stubbly black beard. "That's what we look for here, Jerry. That's what we look for."

Feeling sort of awkward, I thanked him. I mean, what are you supposed to say when someone tells you what excellent hands you've got?

I pushed open the heavy front door and saw Mum waiting in the car. "Good night!" I called, and eagerly ran out of the school, into the snowy evening.

211

After dinner, Mum and Dad insisted that I show them what I had learned in my piano lesson. I didn't really want to. I had only learned that one simple song, and I still hadn't played it all the way through without making any mistakes.

But they forced me into the family room and pushed me onto the piano bench. "If I'm going to pay for the lessons, I want to hear what you're learning," Dad said. He sat down close to Mum on the sofa, facing the back of the piano.

"We only tried one song," I said. "Couldn't we wait till I learn some more?"

"Play it," Dad ordered.

I sighed. "I've got cramp in my hand."

"Come on, Jerry. Don't make excuses," Mum snapped immediately. "Just play the song, okay? Then we won't bug you any more tonight."

"What did the school look like?" Dad asked Mum. "It's right over on the other side of town, isn't it?"

"It's practically *out* of town," Mum told him. "It's in this very old house. Sort of run-down looking, actually. But Jerry told me it's nice inside."

"No, I didn't," I interrupted. "I said it was big. I didn't say it was nice. I got lost in the corridors twice!"

Dad laughed. "I see you have your mother's sense of direction!"

Mum gave Dad a playful shove. "Just play the piece," she said to me.

I found it in the music book and propped the book in front of me on the piano. Then I arranged my fingers on the keys and prepared to play.

But before I hit the first note, the piano erupted with a barrage of low notes. It sounded as if someone was pounding on the keys with both fists.

"Jerry—stop it," Mum said sharply. "That's too loud."

"That can't be what you learned," Dad added.

I put my fingers in place and began to play.

But my notes were drowned out by the horrible, loud banging again.

It sounded like a little kid pounding away on the keys as hard as he could.

"Jerry—give us a *break!*" Mum shouted, holding her ears.

"But I'm not *doing* it!" I screamed. "It isn't *me!*"

18

They didn't believe me.

Instead, they got angry. They accused me of never taking anything seriously, and sent me up to my room.

I was actually glad to get out of the family room and away from that haunted piano. I knew who was pounding the keys and making that racket. The ghost was doing it.

Why? What was she trying to prove?

What did she plan to do to me?

Those questions I couldn't answer . . . yet.

The next Friday afternoon, Mr Toggle kept his promise. He greeted me at the door to the piano school after my mum had dropped me off. He led me through the twisting corridor to his enormous workshop.

Mr Toggle's workshop was the size of a sports hall. The vast room was cluttered with machines and electronic equipment.

An enormous two-headed metal creature, at least three times as tall as the floor sweeper that had terrified me the week before, stood in the centre. It was surrounded by tape machines, stacks of electric motors, cases of tools and strange-looking parts, video equipment, a pile of bicycle wheels, several piano frames with no insides, animal cages, and an old car with its seats removed.

One entire wall seemed to be a control panel. It had more than a dozen video screens, all on, all showing different classes going on in the school. Around the screens were thousands of dials and knobs, blinking red and green lights, speakers, and microphones.

Beneath the control panel, on a counter that ran the length of the room, stood at least a dozen computers. All of them seemed to be powered up.

"Wow!" I exclaimed. My eyes kept darting from one amazing thing to another. "I don't *believe* this!"

Mr Toggle chuckled. His dark eyes lit up. "I find ways to keep busy," he said. He led me to an uncluttered corner of the enormous room. "Let me show you some of my musical instruments."

He walked to a row of tall, grey metal cabinets along the far wall. He pulled a few items from a cabinet and came hurrying back.

"Do you know what this is, Jerry?" He held

up a shiny, brass instrument attached to some kind of tank.

"A saxophone?" I guessed.

"A very special saxophone," he said, grinning. "See? It's attached to this tank of compressed air. That means you don't have to blow into it. You can concentrate on your fingering."

"Wow," I said. "That's really neat."

"Here. Put this on," Mr Toggle urged. He slipped a brown leather cap over my head. The cap had several thin wires flowing out of the back, and it was attached to a small keyboard.

"What is it?" I asked, adjusting the cap over my ears.

"Blink your eyes," Mr Toggle instructed.

I blinked my eyes, and the keyboard played a chord. I moved my eyes from right to left. It played another chord. I winked one eye. It played a note.

"It's completely eye-controlled," Mr Toggle said with pride. "No hands required."

"Wow," I repeated. I didn't know what else to say. This stuff was amazing!

Mr Toggle glanced up at a row of clocks on the control panel wall. "You're late for class, Jerry. Dr Shreek will be waiting. Tell him it's my fault, okay?"

"Okay," I said. "Thanks for showing me everything."

He laughed. "I didn't show you *everything*," he joked. "There's lots more." He rubbed his stubbly beard. "But you'll see it all in due course."

I thanked him again and hurried towards the door. It was nearly four-fifteen. I hoped Dr Shreek wouldn't be angry that I was fifteen minutes late.

As I jogged across the enormous workshop, I nearly ran into a row of dark metal cabinets, shut and padlocked.

Turning away from them, I suddenly heard a voice.

"Help!" A weak cry.

I stopped by the side of the cabinet and listened hard.

And heard it again. A little voice, very faint. "Help me, please!"

"Mr Toggle—what's that?" I cried.

He had begun fiddling with the wires on the brown leather cap. He slowly looked up. "What's *what?*"

"That cry," I told him, pointing to the cabinet. "I heard a voice."

He frowned. "It's just damaged equipment," he muttered, returning his attention to the wires.

"Huh? Damaged equipment?" I wasn't sure I had heard him correctly.

"Yeah. Just some damaged equipment," he repeated immediately. "You'd better hurry, Jerry. Dr Shreek must be wondering where you are."

I heard a second cry. A voice, very weak and tiny. "Help me—please!"

I hesitated. Mr Toggle was staring at me impatiently.

I had no choice. I turned and ran from the

218

room, the weak cries still in my ears.

On Saturday afternoon I went outside to shovel snow off our drive. It had snowed the night before, only a centimetre or two. Now it was one of those clear winter days with a bright blue sky overhead.

It felt good to be out in the crisp air, getting some exercise. Everything seemed so fresh and clean.

I was finishing down at the bottom of the drive, my arms starting to ache from all the shovelling, when I saw Kim Li Chin. She was climbing out of her mother's black Honda, carrying her violin case. I realized she was coming from a lesson.

I had seen her at school a few times, but I hadn't really talked to her since that day she'd run away from me in the corridor.

"Hey!" I called across the street, leaning on the shovel, a little out of breath. "Hi!"

She handed the violin case to her mother and waved back. Then she came jogging towards me, her black hightops crunching over the snow. "How's it going?" she asked. "Pretty snow, huh?"

I nodded. "Yeah. Want to shovel some? I still have to do the path."

She laughed. "No thanks." She had a high, tinkly laugh, like two glasses clinking together.

"You coming from a violin lesson?" I asked, still leaning on the shovel.

"Yeah. I'm working on a Bach piece. It's pretty hard."

"You're ahead of me," I told her. "I'm still doing mostly notes and scales."

Her smile faded. Her eyes grew thoughtful.

We talked for a little while about school. Then I asked if she'd like to come in and have some hot chocolate or something.

"What about the path?" she asked, pointing. "I thought you had to shovel it."

"Dad would be disappointed if I didn't save some of it for him," I joked.

Mum filled two big white mugs with hot chocolate. Of course I burned my tongue on the first sip.

Kim and I were sitting in the family room. Kim sat on the piano bench and tapped some keys lightly. "It has a really good tone," she said, her face growing serious. "Better than my mother's piano."

"Why did you run away that afternoon?" I blurted out.

It had been on my mind ever since it happened. I *had* to know the answer.

She lowered her eyes to the piano keys and pretended she hadn't heard me.

So I asked again. "Why did you run away like that, Kim?"

"I didn't," she replied finally, still avoiding my eyes. "I was late for a lesson, that's all."

I put my hot chocolate mug down on the coffee table and leaned against the arm of the sofa. "I told you I was going to take piano lessons at the Shreek School, remember? Then you got this strange look on your face, and you ran away."

Kim sighed. She had the hot chocolate mug in her lap. I saw that she was gripping it tightly in both hands. "Jerry, I really don't want to talk about it," she said softly. "It's too . . . too scary."

"Scary?" I asked.

"Don't you *know* the stories about the Shreek School?" she asked.

I laughed. I'm not sure why. Maybe it was the serious expression on Kim's face. "Stories? What kind of stories?"

"I really don't want to tell you," she said. She took a long sip from the white mug, then returned it to her lap.

"I've just moved here, remember?" I told her. "So I haven't heard any stories. What are they about?"

"Things about the school," she muttered. She climbed off the piano bench and walked to the window, carrying the mug in one hand.

"What kinds of things?" I demanded. "Come on, Kim—*tell* me!"

"Well . . . things like, there are monsters there," she replied, staring out of the window into my snowy back garden. "Real monsters that live in the basement."

"Monsters?" I laughed.

222

Kim spun round. "It's not funny," she snapped.

"I've *seen* the monsters," I told her, shaking my head.

Her face filled with surprise. "You've *what?*"

"I've seen the monsters," I repeated. "They're floor sweepers."

"Huh?" Her mouth dropped open. She nearly spilled hot chocolate down the front of her sweatshirt. "Floor sweepers?"

"Yeah. Mr Toggle built them. He works at the school. He's some kind of mechanical genius. He builds all kinds of things."

"But—" she started.

"I saw one on my first day at the school," I continued. "I thought it was some kind of monster. It made this weird whining sound, and it was coming right at me. I practically dropped my teeth! But it was one of Mr Toggle's floor cleaners."

Kim tilted her head, staring at me thoughtfully. "Well, you know how stories get started," she said. "I *knew* they probably weren't true. They probably all have simple explanations like that."

"All?" I asked. "Are there more?"

"Well . . ." She hesitated. "There were stories about how kids went in for lessons and never came out again. How they vanished, just disappeared."

"That's impossible," I said.

"Yeah, I suppose so," she agreed quickly.

Then I remembered the tiny voice from the cabinet, calling out for help.

It *had* to be some invention of Mr Toggle's, I told myself. It *had* to be.

Damaged equipment, he'd said. He didn't seem in the least bit excited or upset about it.

"It's funny how scary stories get started," Kim said, walking back to the piano bench.

"Well, the piano school building is creepy and old," I said. "It really looks like some sort of haunted mansion. I suppose that's probably why some of the stories got started."

"Probably," she agreed.

"The school isn't haunted, but that piano is!" I told her. I don't know what made me say it. I hadn't told anyone about the ghost and the piano. I knew no one would believe me.

Kim gave a little start and stared at the piano. "This piano is haunted? What do you mean? How do you know?"

"Late at night, I hear someone playing it," I told her. "A woman. I saw her once."

Kim laughed. "You're having me on—right?"

I shook my head. "No, I'm serious, Kim. I saw this woman. Late at night. She plays the same sad tune over and over again."

"Jerry, come on!" Kim pleaded, rolling her eyes.

"The woman talked to me. Her skin fell off. It—it was so frightening, Kim. Her face disappeared. Her skull, it stared at me. And she warned me to stay away. Stay away."

I felt a shiver. Somehow I had shut that scary scene out of my mind for a few days. But now, as I told it to Kim, it all came back to me.

Kim had a big grin on her face. "You're a better storyteller than I am," she said. "Do you know a lot of ghost stories?"

"*It isn't a story!*" I cried. Suddenly, I was desperate for her to believe me.

Kim started to reply, but my mum poked her head into the living room and interrupted. "Kim, your mum just phoned. She needs you to come home now."

"Suppose I'd better go," Kim said, putting down the hot chocolate mug.

I followed her out.

We had just reached the family room doorway when the piano began to play. A strange jumble of notes.

"See?" I cried excitedly to Kim. "See? *Now* do you believe me?"

We both turned back to stare at the piano.

Bonkers was strutting over the keys, his tail straight up behind him.

Kim laughed. "Jerry, you're funny! I almost believed you!"

"But—but—but—" I spluttered.

That stupid cat had made a fool of me again.

"See you at school," Kim said. "I loved your ghost story."

"Thanks," I said weakly. Then I hurried across the room to chase Bonkers off the piano.

Late that night I heard the piano playing again.

I sat up straight in bed. The shadows on my ceiling seemed to be moving in time to the music.

I had been sleeping lightly, restlessly. I must have kicked off my covers in my sleep, because they were bunched at the foot of the bed.

Now, listening to the familiar slow tune, I was wide awake.

This was not Bonkers strutting over the keys. This was the ghost.

I stood up. The floorboards were ice-cold. Outside the bedroom window, I could see the winter-bare trees shivering in a strong breeze.

As I crept to the bedroom doorway, the music grew louder.

Should I go down there? I asked myself.

Will the ghost disappear the minute I poke my head into the family room?

Do I really want to see her?

I didn't want to see that hideous, grinning skull again.

But I realized I couldn't just stand there in the doorway. I couldn't go back to bed. I couldn't ignore it.

I *had* to go and investigate.

I was pulled downstairs, as if tugged by an invisible rope.

Maybe this time Mum and Dad will hear her, too, I thought as I made my way along the landing. Maybe they will see her, too. Maybe they will finally believe me.

Kim flashed into my mind as I started down the creaking stairs. She thought I was making up a ghost story. She thought I was trying to be funny.

But there really was a ghost in my house, a ghost playing my piano. And I was the only one who knew it.

Into the living room. Across the worn carpet to the dining room.

The music floated so gently, so quietly.

Such ghostly music, I thought . . .

I hesitated just outside the family room doorway. Would she vanish the instant I peeped in?

Was she *waiting* for me?

Taking a deep breath, I took a step into the family room.

She had her head down, her long hair falling over her face.

I couldn't see her eyes.

The piano music seemed to swirl around me, pulling me closer despite my fear.

My legs were trembling, but I took a step closer. Then another.

She was all grey. Shades of grey against the blackness of the night sky through the windows.

Her head bobbed and swayed in rhythm with the music. The sleeves of her blouse billowed as her arms moved over the keys.

I couldn't see her eyes. I couldn't see her face. Her long hair covered her, as if hiding her behind a curtain.

The music soared, so sad, so incredibly sad.

I took a step closer. I suddenly realized I had forgotten to breathe. I let my breath out in a loud *whoosh*.

She stopped playing. Maybe the sound of my

breathing alerted her that I was there.

As she raised her head, I could see her pale eyes peering out at me through her hair.

I didn't move.

I didn't breathe.

I didn't make a sound.

"The stories are true," she whispered. A dry whisper that seemed to come from far away.

I wasn't sure I had heard her correctly. I tried to say something, but my voice caught in my throat.

No sound came out at all.

"The stories are true," she repeated. Her voice was only air, a hiss of air.

I goggled at her.

"Wh-what stories?" I finally managed to choke out.

"The stories about the school," she answered, her hair falling over her face. Then she started to raise her arms off the piano keys. "*They're true*," she moaned. "*The stories are true.*"

She held her arms up to me.

Gaping at them in horror, I cried out—then started to gag.

Her arms ended in stumps. She had no hands.

The next thing I knew, my mum was wrapping her arms around me. "Jerry, calm down. Jerry, it's okay. It's okay," she kept repeating.

"Huh? Mum?"

I was gasping for breath. My chest was heaving up and down. My legs were all wobbly.

"Mum? Where—? How—?"

I looked up to see my dad standing a few metres away, squinting at me through his glasses, his arms crossed in front of his bathrobe. "Jerry, you were screaming loud enough to wake the whole neighbourhood!"

I stared at him in disbelief. I hadn't even realized I was screaming.

"It's okay, now," Mum said soothingly. "It's okay, Jerry. You're okay now."

I'm okay?

Again, I pictured the ghost woman, all in grey, her hair falling down, forming a curtain over her face. Again, I saw her raise her arms to show me.

231

Again, I saw the horrible stumps where her hands should have been.

And again, I heard her dry whisper, "*The stories are true.*"

Why didn't she have any hands? Why?

How could she play the piano without hands?

Why was she haunting my piano? Why did she want to terrify me?

The questions circled my brain so fast, I wanted to scream and scream and scream. But I was all screamed out.

"Your mum and I were both sound asleep. You scared us to death," Dad said. "I've never heard wails like that."

I didn't remember screaming. I didn't remember the ghost disappearing, or Mum and Dad rushing in.

It was too horrifying. I think my mind just shut off.

"I'll make you some hot chocolate," Mum said, still holding me tight. "Try to stop trembling."

"I—I'm trying," I stammered.

"It must have been another nightmare," I heard Dad tell Mum. "A vivid one."

"It wasn't a nightmare!" I shrieked.

"Sorry," Dad said quickly. He didn't want to get me started again.

But it was too late. Before I even realized it was happening, I started to scream. "I don't want to play the piano! Get it out of here! Get it out!"

"Jerry, please—" Mum pleaded, her face tight with alarm.

But I couldn't stop. "I don't want to play! I don't want lessons! I won't go to that piano school! I won't, I *won't!*"

"Okay, okay!" Dad cried, shouting to be heard over my desperate wails. "Okay, Jerry. No one is going to force you."

"Huh?" I gazed from one parent to the other, trying to see if they were serious.

"If you don't want piano lessons, you don't have to take them," Mum said, keeping her voice in a low, soothing tone. "You're only signed up for one more anyway."

"Yeah," Dad quickly joined in. "When you go to the school on Friday, just tell Dr Shreek that it's your last lesson."

"But I don't want—" I started.

Mum put a gentle hand over my mouth. "You have to tell Dr Shreek, Jerry. You can't just give up."

"Tell him on Friday," Dad urged. "You don't have to play the piano if you don't want to. Really."

Mum's eyes searched mine. "Does that make you feel better, Jerry?"

I glanced at the piano, now silent, shimmering dully in the dim light from overhead. "Yeah. I

233

suppose so," I muttered uncertainly. "I suppose it does."

On Friday afternoon after school, a grey, blustery day with dark snowclouds hovering low overhead, Mum drove me to the piano school. She pulled into the long drive between the tall hedges and stopped in front of the entrance to the dark, old building.

I hesitated. "Couldn't I just run in and tell Dr Shreek that I'm not coming any more, then run right back out?"

Mum glanced at the clock on the dashboard. "Take one more lesson, Jerry. It won't hurt. We've already paid for it."

I sighed unhappily. "Will you come in with me? Or can you wait out here for me?"

Mum frowned. "Jerry, I've got three errands to make. I'll be back in an hour, I promise."

Reluctantly, I pushed open the car door. "'Bye, Mum."

"If Dr Shreek asks you why you're giving up lessons, just tell him it was interfering with your schoolwork."

"Okay. See you in an hour," I said. I slammed the car door, then watched as she drove away, the tyres crunching over the gravel drive.

I turned and trudged into the school building.

My trainers thudded loudly as I made my way through the dark corridors to Dr Shreek's room.

I looked for Mr Toggle, but didn't see him. Maybe he was in his enormous workshop inventing more amazing things.

The usual roar of piano notes poured from the practice rooms as I passed by them. Through the small, round windows I could see smiling instructors, their hands waving, keeping the beat, their heads swaying to their pupils' playing.

As I turned a corner and headed down another long, dark corridor, a strange thought popped into my head. I suddenly realized that I had never seen another pupil in the corridors.

I had seen instructors through the windows of the rooms. And I had heard the noise of the pupils' playing. But I had never *seen* another pupil.

Not one.

I didn't have long to think about it. A smiling Dr Shreek greeted me outside the door to our practice room. "How are you today, Jerry?"

"Okay," I replied, following him into the room.

He wore baggy grey trousers held up with bright red braces over a crumpled white shirt. His white hair looked as if it hadn't been brushed in a few days. He gestured for me to take my place on the piano bench.

I sat down quickly, folding my hands tensely in my lap. I wanted to get my speech over with quickly before we began the lesson. "Uh . . . Dr Shreek?"

He walked stiffly across the small room until he was standing right in front of me. "Yes, my boy?" he beamed down at me, his Santa Claus cheeks bright pink.

"Well . . . I . . . this will be my last lesson," I choked out. "I've decided I . . . uh . . . have to give up piano lessons."

His smile vanished. He grabbed my wrist. "Oh, no," he said, lowering his voice to a growl. "No. You're not leaving, Jerry."

"Huh?" I cried.

He tightened his grip on my wrist. He was really hurting me.

"Giving up?" he exclaimed. "Not with those hands." His face twisted into an ugly snarl. "You can't give up, Jerry. I need those beautiful hands."

236

"Let go!" I screamed.

He ignored me and tightened his grip, his eyes narrowing menacingly. "Such excellent hands," he muttered. "Excellent."

"No!"

With a shrill cry, I jerked my wrist free. I leapt up from the piano bench and began running to the door.

"Come back, Jerry!" Dr Shreek called angrily. "You cannot get away!"

He started after me, moving stiffly but steadily, taking long strides.

I pushed open the door and darted out into the corridor. The banging of piano music greeted my ears. The long, dark corridor was empty as always.

"Come back, Jerry!" Dr Shreek called from right behind me.

"No!" I cried out again. I hesitated, trying to decide which way to go, which way led to the front door. Then I lowered my head and started to run.

My trainers thudded over the hard floor. I ran as fast as I could, faster than I'd ever run in my life. The practice rooms whirred past in a dark blur.

But to my surprise, Dr Shreek kept right behind me. "Come back, Jerry," he called, not even sounding out of breath. "Come back. You cannot get away from me."

Glancing back, I saw that he was gaining on me.

I could feel the panic rise in my throat, choking off my air. My legs ached. My heart pounded so hard, it felt as if my chest was about to burst.

I turned a corner and ran down another long corridor.

Where was I? Was I heading towards the front door?

I couldn't tell. This dark corridor looked like all the others.

Maybe Dr Shreek is right. Maybe I *can't* get away, I thought, feeling the blood throb at my temples as I turned another corner.

I searched for Mr Toggle. Perhaps he could save me. But the corridors were empty. Piano music poured out of every room, but no one was out in the corridor.

"Come back, Jerry! There's no use running!"

"Mr Toggle!" I screamed, my voice hoarse and breathless. "Mr Toggle—help me! Help me, please!"

I turned another corner, my trainers sliding on the smoothly polished floor. I was gasping for breath now, my chest heaving.

I saw double doors up ahead. Did they lead to the front?

I couldn't remember.

With a low moan, I stuck out both hands and pushed open the doors.

"No!" I heard Dr Shreek shout behind me. "No, Jerry! Don't go into the recital hall!"

Too late.

I pushed through the doors and bolted inside. Still running, I found myself in an enormous, brightly lit room.

I took a few more steps—then stopped in horror.

The piano music was deafening—like a never-ending roar of thunder.

At first, the room was a blur. Then it slowly began to come into focus.

I saw row after row of black pianos. Beside each piano stood a smiling instructor. The instructors all looked alike. They were all bobbing their heads in time to the music.

The music was being played by—

It was being played by—

I gasped, staring from row to row.

**The music was being played by—*HANDS*!
Human hands floating over the keyboards.
No people attached.
Just *HANDS*!**

My eyes darted down the rows of pianos. A pair of hands floated above each piano.

The instructors were all bald-headed men in grey suits with smiles plastered onto their faces. Their heads bobbed and swayed, their grey eyes opened and closed as the hands played over the keys.

Hands.

Just hands.

As I gaped, paralysed, trying to make sense of what I saw, Dr Shreek burst into the room from behind me. He made a running dive at my legs, trying to tackle me.

Somehow I dodged away from his out-stretched hands.

He groaned and hit the floor on his stomach. I watched him slide across the smooth floor, his face red with anger.

Then I spun round, away from the dozens of hands, away from the banging pianos, and started back towards the doors.

But Dr Shreek was faster than I imagined. To my surprise, he was on his feet in a second, moving quickly to block my escape.

I skidded to a stop.

I tried to turn round, to get away from him. But I lost my balance and fell.

The piano music swirled around me. I looked up to see the rows of hands pounding away on their keyboards.

With a frightened gasp, I struggled to my feet.

Too late.

Dr Shreek was closing in on me, a gleeful smile of triumph on his red, round face.

"No!" I cried, and tried to climb to my feet.

But Dr Shreek bent over me, grabbed my left ankle, and held on. "You can't get away, Jerry," he said calmly, not even out of breath.

"Let me go! Let me go!" I tried to twist out of his grip. But he was surprisingly strong. I couldn't free myself.

"Help me! Somebody—help me!" I cried, screaming over the roar of the pianos.

"I need your hands, Jerry," Dr Shreek said. "Such beautiful hands."

"You can't! You *can't!*" I shrieked.

The double doors burst open.

Mr Toggle ran in, his expression confused. His eyes darted quickly around the enormous room.

"Mr Toggle!" I cried happily. "Mr Toggle— help me! He's *crazy!* Help me!"

Mr Toggle's mouth dropped open in surprise. "Don't worry, Jerry!" he called.

243

"Help me! Hurry!" I screamed.

"Don't worry!" he repeated.

"Jerry, you can't get away!" Dr Shreek cried, holding me down on the floor.

Struggling to free myself, I watched Mr Toggle run to the far wall. He pulled open a grey metal door, revealing some kind of control panel.

"Don't worry!" he called to me.

I saw him pull a switch on the control panel.

Instantly, Dr Shreek's hand loosened.

I pulled my leg free and scrambled to my feet, panting hard.

Dr Shreek slumped into a heap. His hands drooped lifelessly to his sides. His eyes closed. His head sank, his chin lowering to his chest.

He didn't move.

He's some kind of robot, I saw to my amazement.

"Are you okay, Jerry?" Mr Toggle had hurried to my side.

I suddenly realized my entire body was trembling. The piano music roared inside my head. The room began to spin.

I held my hands over my ears, trying to shut out the pounding noise. "Make them stop! Tell them to stop!" I cried.

Mr Toggle jogged back to the control panel and threw another switch.

The music stopped. The hands froze in place

over their keyboards. The instructors stopped bobbing their heads.

"Robots. All robots," I murmured, still shaking.

Mr Toggle hurried back, his dark eyes studying me. "Are you okay?"

"Dr Shreek—he's a robot," I uttered in a trembling whisper. If only I could get my knees to stop shaking!

"Yes, he's my best creation," Mr Toggle declared, smiling. He placed a hand on Dr Shreek's still shoulder. "He's really life-like, isn't he?"

"They—they're *all* robots," I whispered, motioning to the instructors, frozen beside their pianos.

Mr Toggle nodded. "Primitive ones," he said, still leaning on Dr Shreek. "They're not as advanced as my buddy Dr Shreek here."

"You—made them all?" I asked.

Mr Toggle nodded, smiling. "Every one of them."

I couldn't stop shaking. I was starting to feel really sick. "Thanks for stopping him. I think Dr Shreek was out of control or something. I—I've got to go now," I said weakly. I started walking towards the double doors, forcing my trembling knees to cooperate.

"Not just yet," Mr Toggle said, placing a gentle hand on my shoulder.

245

"Huh?" I turned to face him.

"You can't leave just yet," he said, his smile fading. "I need your hands, you see."

"What?"

He pointed to a piano against the wall. A grey-suited instructor stood lifelessly beside it, a smile frozen on his face. There were no hands suspended over the keyboard.

"That will be *your* piano, Jerry," Mr Toggle said.

I started backing towards the double doors one step at a time. "Wh-why?" I stammered. "Why do you need my hands?"

"Human hands are too hard to build, too complicated, too many parts," Mr Toggle replied. He scratched his black, stubbly beard with one hand as he moved towards me.

"But—" I started, taking another step back.

"I can make the hands play beautifully," Mr Toggle explained, his eyes locked on mine. "I've designed computer programmes to make them play more beautifully than any live human can play. But I can't build hands. The pupils must supply the hands."

"But *why*?" I demanded. "Why are you *doing* this?"

"To make beautiful music, naturally," Mr Toggle replied, taking another step closer. "I love beautiful music, Jerry. And music is so much more beautiful, so much more *perfect*, when human mistakes don't get in the way."

He took another step towards me. Then another. "You understand, don't you?" His dark eyes burned into mine.

"No!" I screamed. "No, I *don't* understand! You can't have my hands! You can't!"

I took another step back. My legs were still trembling.

If I can just get through those doors, I thought, maybe I have a chance. Maybe I can outrun him. Maybe I can get out of this crazy building.

It was my only hope.

Gathering my strength, ignoring the pounding of my heart, I turned.

I darted towards the doors.

"Ohh!" I cried out as the ghost woman appeared in front of me.

The woman from my house, from my piano.

She rose up, all in grey except for her eyes. Her eyes glowed red as fire. Her mouth was twisted in an ugly snarl of rage. She floated towards me, blocking my path to the door.

I'm trapped, I realized.

Trapped between Mr Toggle and the ghost.

There's no escape now.

"*I warned you!*" the ghost woman wailed, her red eyes glowing with fury. "*I warned you!*"

"No, please—" I managed to cry in a choked voice. I raised my hands in front of me, trying to shield myself from her. "Please—let me go!"

To my surprise, she floated right past me.

She was glaring at Mr Toggle, I realized.

He staggered back, his face tight with terror.

The ghost woman raised her arms. "*Awaken!*" she wailed. "*Awaken!*"

And as she waved her arms, I saw a fluttering at the pianos. The fluttering became a mist. Wisps of grey cloud rose up from each piano.

I backed away to the doors, my eyes wide with disbelief.

At each piano, the dark mist took shape.

They were ghosts, I realized.

Ghosts of boys, girls, men, and women.

249

I watched, frozen in horror, as they rose up and claimed their hands. They moved their fingers, testing their hands.

And then, with arms outstretched, their hands fluttering in front of them, the ghosts floated away from their pianos, moving in rows, in single file, towards Mr Toggle.

"No! Get away! Get away!" Mr Toggle shrieked.

He turned and tried to flee through the doors. But I blocked his path.

And the ghosts swarmed all over him.

Their hands pulled him down. Their hands pressed him to the floor.

He kicked and struggled and screamed.

"Let me up! Get off me! Get off!"

But the hands, dozens and dozens of hands, flattened over him, held him down, pushed him face-down on the floor.

The grey ghost woman turned to me. "*I tried to warn you!*" she called over Mr Toggle's frantic screams. "*I tried to scare you away! I lived in your house. I was a victim of this school! I tried to frighten you from becoming a victim, too!*"

"I—I—"

"*Run!*" she ordered. "*Hurry—call for help!*"

But I was frozen in place, too shocked by what I was seeing to move.

As I stared in disbelief, the ghostly hands

swarmed over Mr Toggle and lifted him off the floor. He squirmed and struggled, but he couldn't free himself from their powerful grasp.

They carried him to the door and then out. I followed them to the doorway to watch.

Mr Toggle appeared to be floating, floating into the deep woods beside the school. The hands carried him away. He disappeared into the tangled trees.

I knew he'd never be seen again.

I spun round to thank the ghost woman for trying to warn me.

But she had gone, too.

I was all alone now.

The corridor stretched behind me in eerie silence. Ghostly silence.

The piano music had ended . . . forever.

A few weeks later, my life had pretty much returned to normal.

Dad put an ad in the newspaper and sold the piano straight away to a family on the other side of town. It left a space in the family room, so Mum and Dad got a big-screen TV!

I never saw the ghost woman again. Maybe she moved out with the piano. I don't know.

I made some good friends and was starting to get used to my new school. I was thinking seriously of trying out for the baseball team. I'm not a great hitter, but I'm good in the field. Everyone says I have great hands.

Be Careful What You Wish For

Judith Bellwood deliberately tripped me up in maths class.

I saw her white trainer shoot out into the aisle. Too late.

I was carrying my notebook up to the blackboard to put a problem on it. My eyes were on the scrawls in my notebook. I'm not the neatest writer in the world.

And before I could stop, I saw the white trainer shoot out. I tripped over it and went sprawling to the floor, landing hard on my elbows and knees. Of course all the papers flew out of my notebook and scattered everywhere.

And the whole class thought it was a riot. Everyone was laughing and cheering as I struggled to pull myself up. Judith and her friend, Anna Frost, laughed hardest of all.

I landed on my funny bone, and the pain vibrated up and down my whole body. As I climbed to my feet and then bent to pick up my notebook papers, I knew my face was as red as a tomato.

"Nice move, Sam!" Anna yelled, a big grin on her face.

"Instant replay!" someone else shouted.

I glanced up to see a triumphant glow in Judith's green eyes.

I'm the tallest girl in my seventh-grade class. No. Correct that. I'm the tallest *kid* in my seventh-grade class. I'm at least two inches taller than my friend, Cory Blinn, and he's the tallest boy.

I'm also the clumsiest person who ever stumbled over the face of the earth. I mean, just because I'm tall and slender doesn't mean I have to be graceful. And believe me, I'm not.

But why is it such a riot when I stumble over a bin or drop my tray in the cafeteria or trip over someone's foot in the maths lesson?

Judith and Anna are just cruel, that's all.

I know they both call me "Stork" behind my back. Cory told me they do.

And Judith is always making fun of my name, which is Byrd. Samantha Byrd. *"Why don't you fly away, Byrd!"* That's what she's always saying to me. Then she and Anna laugh as if that's the funniest joke they've ever heard.

"Why don't you fly away, Byrd!"

Ha-ha. Big joke.

Cory says that Judith is just jealous of me. But

that's stupid. I mean, why should Judith be jealous? She's not nine feet tall. She's about five-two, perfect for a twelve-year-old. She's graceful. She's athletic. And she's really pretty, with pale, creamy skin, big green eyes, and wavy, copper-coloured hair down to her shoulders.

So what's there to be jealous about?

I think Cory is just trying to make me feel better—and doing a *lousy* job of it.

Anyway, I gathered all my papers together and shoved them back into the notebook. Sharon asked if I was okay. (Sharon is my teacher. We call all the teachers by their first names here at Montrose Middle School.)

I muttered that I was fine, even though my elbow was throbbing like mad. And I copied the problem on to the board.

The chalk squeaked, and everyone groaned and complained. I can't help it. I've never been able to write on the board without squeaking the chalk.

It isn't *such* a big deal—*is* it?

I heard Judith whisper some joke about me to Anna, but I couldn't hear what it was. I glanced up from the problem to see the two of them sniggering and smirking at me.

And wouldn't you know it—I couldn't solve the problem. I had something wrong with the equation, and I couldn't figure out what it was.

Sharon stepped up behind me, her skinny

arms crossed over her ugly lime-green sweater. She moved her lips as she read what I had written, trying to see where I had gone wrong.

And of course Judith raised her hand and called out, "I see the problem, Sharon. Byrd can't add. Four and two is six, not five."

I could feel myself blushing again.

Where would I be without Judith to point out my mistakes to the whole class?

Everyone was laughing again. Even Sharon thought it was funny.

And I had to stand there and take it. Good old Samantha, the class fool. The class idiot.

My hand was shaking as I erased my stupid mistake and wrote in the right numbers.

I was *so angry*. At Judith. And at myself.

But I kept it together as I walked—carefully—back to my seat. I didn't even glance at Judith as I walked past her.

I kept it together until Home Economics lesson that afternoon.

Then it got ugly.

Daphne is our teacher in Home Economics. I like Daphne. She is a big, jolly woman with several chins and a great sense of humour.

The rumour is that Daphne always makes us bake cakes and pies and brownies so that she can eat them all after we leave the lesson.

That's a little bit mean, I think. But it's probably a little bit true.

We have Home Economics right after lunch, so we're never very hungry. Most of what we make wouldn't make good *dog food*, anyway. So it mostly gets left in the Home Economics classroom.

I always look forward to the lesson. Partly because Daphne is a fun teacher. And partly because it's the one lesson where there's no homework.

The only bad thing about the Home Economics lesson is that Judith is in it, too.

Judith and I had a little run-in in the cafeteria.

I sat down at the far end of the table, as far away from her as I could get. But I still heard her telling a couple of eighth-graders, "Byrd tried to fly in the maths lesson."

Everyone laughed and stared at me.

"You tripped me, Judith!" I shouted angrily. My mouth was full of egg salad, which dribbled down my chin when I shouted.

And everyone laughed at me again.

Judith said something, which I couldn't hear over all the noise in the cafeteria. She smirked at me and tossed her red hair behind her shoulders.

I started to get up and go over to her. I don't know *what* I was thinking of doing. But I was so angry, I wasn't thinking too clearly.

Luckily, Cory appeared across the table. He dropped his lunch down on the table, turned the chair around backwards the way he always does, and sat down.

"What's four plus two?" he teased.

"Forty-two," I replied, rolling my eyes. "Do you *believe* Judith?" I asked bitterly.

"Of course I believe Judith," he said, pulling open his brown lunchbag. "Judith is Judith."

"What's that supposed to mean?" I snapped.

He shrugged. A grin broke out across his face. "I don't know."

Cory is kind of cute. He has dark brown eyes that sort of crinkle up in the corners, a nose that's a little too long, and a funny, crooked smile.

He has great hair, but he never brushes it. So he never takes off his cap. It's an Orlando Magic cap, even though he doesn't know or care about the team. He just likes the cap.

He peeked into his lunchbag and made a face.

"Again?" I asked, wiping egg salad off the front of my T-shirt with a napkin.

"Yeah. Again," he replied glumly. He pulled out the same lunch his father packed for him every single morning. A toasted cheese sandwich and an orange. "Yuck!"

"Why does your dad give you toasted cheese every day?" I asked. "Didn't you tell him it gets cold and slimy by lunchtime?"

"I told him," Cory groaned, picking up one half of the sandwich in one hand and examining it as if it were some sort of science lab specimen. "He said it's good protein."

"How can it be good protein if you throw it in the bin every day?" I asked.

Cory grinned his crooked grin. "I didn't tell him that I throw it in the bin every day." He shoved the rubbery sandwich back into the bag and started to peel the orange.

"It's a good thing you came by," I said, swallowing the last bite of my egg salad sandwich. "I was about to get up and murder Judith over there."

261

We both glanced down the table. Judith and the two eighth-graders had their chairs tilted back and were laughing about something. One of the eighth-graders had a magazine, *People* magazine, I think, and she was showing a picture in it to the others.

"Don't murder Judith," Cory advised, still peeling the orange. "You'll get into trouble."

I laughed, scornful laughter. "You kidding? I'd get an award."

"If you murder Judith, your basketball team will never win another game," Cory said, concentrating on the orange.

"Ooh, that's cruel!" I exclaimed. I tossed my screwed-up aluminium foil at him. It bounced off his chest and dropped on to the floor.

He was right, of course. Judith was the best player on our team, the Montrose Mustangs. She was the *only* good player. She could dribble really well without getting the ball tangled up in her legs. And she had a great shooting eye.

I, of course, was the *worst* player on the team.

I admit it. I'm really clumsy, as I've said, which doesn't get you very far on the basketball court.

I really hadn't wanted to be on the Mustangs. I knew I'd stink.

But Ellen insisted. Ellen is the girls' basketball coach. Ellen insisted I be on the team.

"Sam, you're so tall!" she told me. "You've *got*

to play basketball. You're a natural!"

Sure, I'm a natural. Naturally clumsy.

I can't shoot at all, not even foul shots. *Especially* not foul shots.

And I can't run without tripping over my own Reeboks. And my hands are small, even though the rest of me isn't, so I'm not too good at passing or catching the ball.

I think Ellen has learned her lesson: *tall ain't all.*

But now she's too embarrassed to take me off the team. And I keep at it. I work hard at practice. I mean, I keep thinking I'll get better. I couldn't get any worse.

If only Judith wasn't such a hotshot.

And if only she was nicer to me.

But, as Cory put it, "Judith is Judith." She's always yelling at me during practice, and making fun of me, and making me feel two feet tall (which I sometimes wish I were!)

"Byrd, why don't you give us a break and fly away!"

If she says that one more time, I'll punch her lights out. I really will.

"What are you thinking about, Sam?" Cory's voice broke into my bitter thoughts.

"About Judith, of course," I muttered. "Miss Perfect."

"Hey, stop," he said, pulling apart the orange sections. "You have good qualities, too, you know."

"Oh, really?" I snapped. "What are my good qualities? That I'm tall?"

"No." He finally popped an orange section into his mouth. I never saw anyone take so long to eat an orange! "You're also clever," he said. "And you're funny."

"Thanks a lot," I replied, frowning.

"And you're very generous," he added. "You're so generous, you're going to give me that bag of crisps, right?" He pounced on it before I could grab it away from him.

I *knew* there was a reason for his compliments.

I watched Cory stuff down my crisps. He didn't even offer me one.

Then the bell rang and I hurried to Home Economics.

Where I completely lost it.

What happened was this: we were making tapioca pudding. And it was really messy.

We all had big orange mixing bowls, and the ingredients were spread out on the long table next to the oven.

I was busily stirring mine. It was nice and gloppy, and it made this great *glop glop* sound as I stirred it with a long wooden spoon.

My hands were sticky for some reason. I had probably spilled some of the pudding on to them. So I stopped to wipe them on my apron.

I was being pretty neat—for me. There were

264

only a few yellow puddles of pudding on my table. Most of it was actually in the mixing bowl.

I finished stirring and, when I looked up, there was Judith.

I was a little surprised because she had been working on the other side of the room by the windows. We generally keep as far apart from each other as possible.

Judith had this odd smile on her face. And as she approached me, she pretended to trip.

I *swear* she only pretended to trip!

And she spilled her whole mixing bowl of tapioca on to my shoes.

My brand-new blue Doc Martens.

"Oops!" she said.

That's all. Just "Oops".

I looked down at my brand-new shoes covered in gloppy yellow pudding.

And that's when I lost it.

I uttered an angry roar and went for Judith's throat.

I didn't plan it or anything. I think it was temporary insanity.

I just reached out both hands and grabbed Judith by the throat, and began to strangle her.

I mean, they were *brand-new shoes*!

Judith started struggling and tried to scream. She pulled my hair and tried to scratch me.

But I held on to her throat and roared again, like an angry tiger.

And Daphne had to pull us apart.

She pulled me away by the shoulders, then thrust her wide body between us, blocking our view of each other.

I was panting loudly. My chest was heaving up and down.

"Samantha! Samantha! What were you *doing*?" I *think* that's what Daphne was screaming.

I couldn't really hear her. I had this roaring in my ears, loud as a waterfall. I think it was just my anger.

Before I knew it, I had pushed myself away from the table and was running out of the room. I ran out into the empty hall—and stopped.

I didn't know what to do next. I was *so* angry.

If I had three wishes, I told myself, I know what they would be: destroy Judith! Destroy Judith! Destroy Judith!

Little did I know that I would soon get my wish.

All three of them.

266

Daphne made Judith and me shake hands and apologize to each other after she dragged me back into the classroom. I had to do it. It was either that or be thrown out of school.

"It really was an accident," Judith muttered under her breath. "What's your problem, Byrd?"

Not much of an apology, if you ask me.

But I shook hands with her. I didn't need my parents being called to school because their daughter had tried to strangle a classmate.

And I showed up—reluctantly—for basketball practice after school. I knew if I didn't show, Judith would tell everyone that she had scared me away.

I showed up because I knew Judith didn't want me to. Which I think is as good a reason as any.

Also, I needed the exercise. I needed to run back and forth across the court a few hundred times to get the anger out. I needed to sweat out the frustration from not being able to finish strangling Judith.

"Let's do some fast laps," Ellen suggested.

Some of the other girls groaned, but I didn't. I started running before Ellen even blew her whistle.

We were all in shorts and sleeveless T-shirts. Ellen wore a grey tracksuit that was baggy in all the wrong places. She had frizzy red hair, and she was so straight and skinny, she looked sort of like a match.

Ellen wasn't very athletic. She told us she coached girls' basketball because they paid her extra, and she needed the money.

After running our laps around the gym, practice went pretty much as usual.

Judith and Anna passed the ball to each other a lot. And they both took a lot of shots—jump shots, lay-ups, even hook shots.

The others tried to keep up with them.

I tried not to be noticed.

I was still simmering about the tapioca pudding disaster and wanted as little contact with Judith—or *anyone*—as possible. I mean, I was really feeling glum.

And watching Judith sink a twenty-foot jumper, catch her own rebound, and scoop a perfect two-handed shovel pass to Anna wasn't helping to cheer me up one bit.

Of course, things got worse.

Anna actually passed the ball to me. I muffed it. It bounced off my hands, hit me in the forehead, and rolled away.

"Heads up, Byrd!" I heard Ellen cry.

I kept running. I tried not to look upset that I had blown my first opportunity of the practice.

A few minutes later, I saw the ball flying towards me again, and I heard Judith shout, "Get this one, Stork!"

I was so startled that she had called me "Stork" to my face that I *caught* the ball. I started to dribble to the basket—and Anna reached a hand in and easily stole the ball. She spun around and sent an arching shot to the basket, which nearly went in.

"Nice steal, Anna!" Ellen cried.

Breathing hard, I turned angrily to Judith. "What did you call me?"

Judith pretended she didn't hear me.

Ellen blew the whistle. "Time out!" she shouted.

We practised fast breaks three at a time. Dribbling fast, we'd pass the ball back and forth. Then the one under the hoop with the ball was supposed to take the shot.

I need to practise *slow* breaks! I thought to myself.

I had no trouble keeping up with the others. I mean, I had the longest legs, after all. I could run

269

fast enough. I just couldn't do anything else while I was running.

As Judith, Anna, and I came roaring down the court, I prayed I wouldn't make a total fool of myself. Sweat poured down my forehead. My heart was racing.

I took a short pass from Anna, dribbled under the basket, and took a shot. The ball flew straight up in the air, then bounced back to the floor. It didn't even come close to the backboard.

I could hear girls laughing on the sidelines. Judith and Anna had their usual superior smirks on their faces. "Good eye!" Judith called, and everyone laughed some more.

After twenty minutes of fast-break torture, Ellen blew her whistle. "Scrimmage," she called out. That was the signal for us to divide into two teams and play each other.

I sighed, wiping perspiration off my forehead with the back of my hand. I tried to get into the game. I concentrated hard, mainly on not messing up. But I was pretty discouraged.

Then, a few minutes into the game, Judith and I both dived for the ball at the same time.

Somehow, as I dived, my arms outstretched, Judith's knee came up hard—and plunged like a knife into my chest.

The pain shot through my entire body.

I tried to cry out. But I couldn't make a sound.

I uttered a weird, gasping noise, sort of like the

270

honk of a sick seal—and realized I couldn't breathe.

Everything turned red. Bright, shimmering red.

Then black.

I knew I was going to die.

Having your breath knocked out of you has to be the worst feeling in the world. It's just so scary. You try to breathe, and you can't. And the pain just keeps swelling, like a balloon being blown up right inside your chest.

I really thought I was dead meat.

Of course I was perfectly okay a few minutes later. I still felt a little shaky, a little dizzy. But I was basically okay.

Ellen insisted that one of the girls walk me to the changing room. Naturally, Judith volunteered. As we walked, she apologized. She said it had been an accident. A total accident.

I didn't say anything. I didn't want her to apologize. I didn't want to talk to her at all. I just wanted to strangle her again.

This time for good.

I mean, how much can one girl take in a day? Judith had tripped me in the maths lesson, dumped her disgusting tapioca pudding all over my new Doc Martens in Home Economics, and kicked me unconscious in basketball practice.

Did I really have to smile and accept her apology now?

No way! No way in a million years.

I trudged silently to the changing room, my head bent, my eyes on the floor.

When she saw that I wasn't going to buy her cheap apology, Judith got angry. *Do you believe that?* She shoves her knee through my chest—then *she* gets angry!

"Why don't you just fly away, Byrd!" she muttered. Then she went trotting back to the gym floor.

I got changed without showering. Then I collected my stuff, and slunk out of the building, and got my bike.

That's really the last straw, I thought, walking my bike across the car park at the back of school.

It was about half an hour later. The late afternoon sky was grey and overcast. I felt a few light drops of rain on my head.

The last straw, I repeated to myself.

I live two streets away from the school, but I didn't feel like going home. I felt like riding and riding and riding. I felt like just going straight and never turning back.

I was angry and upset and shaky. But mainly angry.

Ignoring the raindrops, I climbed on to my bike and began pedalling in the direction away from my house. Front gardens and houses went by in a whir. I didn't see them. I didn't see anything.

I pedalled harder and harder. It felt so good to get away from school. To get away from Judith.

The rain started to come down a little harder. I didn't mind. I raised my face to the sky as I pedalled. The raindrops felt cold and refreshing on my hot skin.

When I looked down, I saw that I had reached Jeffers' Woods, a long stretch of trees that divides my neighbourhood from the next.

A narrow bike path twisted through the tall, old trees, which were winter-bare and looked sort of sad and lonely without their leaves. Sometimes I took the path, seeing how fast I could ride over its curves and bumps.

But the sky was darkening, the black clouds hovering lower. And I saw a glimmering streak of lightning in the sky over the trees.

I decided I'd better turn around and ride home.

But as I turned, someone stepped in front of me.

A woman!

I gasped, startled to see someone on this empty road by the woods.

I squinted at her as the rain began to fall harder, pattering on the pavement around me.

She wasn't young, and she wasn't old. She had dark eyes, like two black coals, on a pale, white face. Her thick, black hair flowed loosely behind her.

Her clothing was sort of old-fashioned. She had a bright red, heavy woollen shawl pulled around her shoulders. She wore a long black skirt down to her ankles.

Her dark eyes seemed to light up as she met my stare.

She looked confused.

I should have pedalled away from her as fast as I could.

If only I had known . . .

But I didn't flee. I didn't escape.

Instead, I smiled at her. "Can I help you?" I asked.

The woman's eyes narrowed. I could see she was checking me out.

I lowered my feet to the ground, balancing the bike between my legs. The rain pattered on the pavement, big cold drops.

I suddenly remembered I had a hood on my anorak. So I reached up behind my head and slipped it over my hair.

The sky darkened to an eerie olive colour. The bare trees in the woods shivered in a swirling breeze.

The woman took a few steps closer. She was so pale, I thought. Almost ghostlike, except for the deep, dark eyes that were staring so hard at me.

"I—I seem to have lost my way," she said. To my surprise, she had an old woman's voice, sort of shaky and frail.

I squinted at her from under my hood. The rain was matting her thick, black hair to her head. It

276

was impossible to tell how old she was. She could have been twenty or sixty!

"This is Montrose Avenue," I told her, speaking loudly because of the drumming of the raindrops. "Actually, Montrose ends here. At the woods."

She nodded thoughtfully, pursing her pale lips. "I am trying to get to Madison Road," she said. "I think I have completely lost my direction."

"You're quite far from Madison Road," I said. "It's way over there." I pointed.

She chewed at her lower lip. "I'm usually quite good at directions," she said fretfully in her shaky voice. She adjusted the heavy red shawl over her slender shoulders.

"Madison Road is way over on the east side of town," I said with a shiver. The rain was cold. I was eager to go home and get into some dry clothes.

"Can you take me there?" the woman asked. She grabbed my wrist.

I almost gasped out loud. Her hand was as cold as ice!

"Can you take me there?" she repeated, bringing her face close to mine. "I would be ever so grateful."

She had taken her hand away. But I could still feel the icy grip on my wrist.

Why didn't I run away?

Why didn't I raise my feet to the pedals and ride out of there as fast as I could?

"Sure. I'll show you where it is," I said.

"Thank you, dear." She smiled. She had a dimple in one cheek when she smiled. I realized she was kind of pretty, in an old-fashioned way.

I climbed off my bike and, holding on to the handlebars, began to walk it. The woman stepped beside me, adjusting her shawl. She walked in the middle of the street, her eyes trained on me.

The rain continued to come down. I saw another jagged bolt of lightning far away in the olive sky. The swirling wind made my anorak flap against my legs.

"Am I going too fast?" I asked.

"No, dear. I can keep up," she replied with a smile. She had a small purple bag slung over her shoulder. She protected the bag by tucking it under her arm.

She wore black boots under her long skirt. The boots, I saw, had tiny buttons running up the sides. The boots clicked on the wet pavement as we walked.

"I am sorry to be so much trouble," the woman said, again pursing her lips fretfully.

"No trouble," I replied. My good deed for the day, I thought, brushing a drop of rain off my nose.

"I love the rain," she said, raising her hands to it, letting the raindrops splash upon her open

278

palms. "Without the rain, what would wash the evil away?"

That's a weird thing to say, I thought. I muttered a reply. I wondered what evil she was talking about.

Her long, black hair was completely soaked, but she didn't seem to mind. She walked quickly with long, steady strides, swinging one hand as she walked, protecting the purple bag under the other arm.

A few streets later, the handlebars slipped out of my hands. My bike toppled over, and the pedal scraped my knee as I tried to grab the bike before it fell.

What a fool!

I pulled the bike up and began walking it again. My knee throbbed. I shivered. The wind blew the rain into my face.

What am I doing out here? I asked myself.

The woman kept walking quickly, a thoughtful expression on her face. "It's quite a storm," she said, gazing up at the dark clouds. "This is so nice of you, dear."

"It isn't too far out of my way," I said politely. *Just eight or ten streets!*

"I don't know how I could have gone so far astray," she said, shaking her head. "I was sure I was headed in the right direction. Then when I came to those woods . . ."

"We're almost there," I said.

"What is your name?" she asked suddenly.

"Samantha," I told her. "But everyone calls me Sam."

"My name is Clarissa," she offered. "I'm the Crystal Woman."

I wasn't sure I'd heard that last part correctly. I puzzled over it, then let it slip from my mind.

It was late, I realized. Mum and Dad might already be home from work. Even if they weren't, my brother, Ron, was probably home, wondering where I was.

A car rolled towards us, its headlights on. I shielded my eyes from the bright lights and nearly dropped my bike again.

The woman was still walking in the centre of the street. I moved towards the kerb so she could move out of the car's path. But she didn't seem to care about it. She kept walking straight, her expression not changing, even though the bright headlights were in her face.

"Look out!" I cried.

I don't know if she heard me.

The car swerved to avoid her and honked its horn as it rolled by.

She smiled warmly at me as we kept walking. "So good of you to care about a total stranger," she said.

The streetlights flashed on suddenly. They made the wet street glow. The bushes and hedges, the grass, the pavements—everything seemed to glow. It all looked unreal.

"Here we are. This is Madison Road," I said, pointing to the street sign. *Finally!* I thought.

I just wanted to say goodbye to this strange woman and pedal home as fast as I could.

Lightning flickered. Closer this time.

What a dreary day, I thought with a sigh.

Then I remembered Judith.

The whole miserable day suddenly rolled through my mind again. I felt a wave of anger sweep over me.

"Which way is east?" the woman asked, her shaky voice breaking into my bitter thoughts.

"East?" I gazed both ways down Madison Road, trying to clear Judith from my mind. I pointed.

The wind picked up suddenly, blowing a sheet of rain against me. I tightened the grip on the handlebars.

"You are so kind," the woman said, wrapping the shawl around her. Her dark eyes stared hard into mine. "So kind. Most young people aren't kind like you."

"Thank you," I replied awkwardly. The cold made me shiver again. "Well . . . goodbye." I started to climb on to my bike.

"No. Wait," she pleaded. "I want to repay you."

"Huh?" I uttered. "No. Really. You don't have to."

"I want to repay you," the woman insisted.

She grabbed my wrist again. And again I felt a shock of cold.

"You've been so kind," the woman repeated. "So kind to a total stranger."

I tried to free my wrist, but her grip was surprisingly tight. "You don't have to thank me," I said.

"I want to repay you," she replied, bringing her face close to mine, still holding on to my wrist. "Tell you what. I'll grant you three wishes."

She's crazy, I realized.

I stared into those coal black eyes. Rainwater trickled from her hair, down the sides of her pale face. I could feel the coldness of her hand, even through the sleeve of my anorak.

The woman is *crazy*, I thought.

I've been walking through the pouring rain for twenty minutes with a crazy person.

"Three wishes," the woman repeated, lowering her voice as if not wanting to be overheard by anyone.

"No. Thanks. I've really got to get home," I said. I tugged my wrist from her grasp and turned to my bike.

"I'll grant you three wishes," the woman repeated. "Anything you wish for shall come true." She moved the purple bag in front of her and carefully pulled something from it. It was a glass ball, bright red, the size of a large grape-fruit. It sparkled despite the darkness around us.

"That's nice of you," I said, wiping water off the bike seat with my hand. "But I don't really have any wishes right now."

"Please—let me repay you for your kindness," the woman insisted. She raised the gleaming red ball in one hand. Her hand was small and as pale as her face, the fingers bony. "I really do want to repay you."

"My—uh—mum will be worried," I said, glancing up and down the street.

No one in sight.

No one to protect me from this lunatic if she turned dangerous.

Just how crazy was she? I wondered. Could she be dangerous? Was I making her angry by not playing along, by not making a wish?

"It isn't a joke," the woman said, reading the doubt in my eyes. "Your wishes will come true. I promise you." She narrowed her gaze. The red ball suddenly glowed brighter. "Make your first wish, Samantha."

I stared back at her, thinking hard. I was cold and wet and hungry—and a little frightened. I just wanted to get home and get dry.

What if she won't let me go?

What if I can't get rid of her? What if she follows me home?

Again, I searched up and down the street. Most of the houses had lights on. I could probably run to the nearest one and get help if I needed it.

284

But, I decided, it might be easier just to play along with the crazy woman and make a wish.

Maybe that would satisfy her, and she'd go on her way and let me go home.

"What is your wish, Samantha?" she demanded. Her black eyes glowed red, the same colour as the gleaming ball in her hand.

She suddenly looked very old. Ancient. Her skin was so pale and tight, I thought I could see her skull underneath.

I froze.

I couldn't think of a wish.

And then I blurted out, "My wish is . . . to be the strongest player on my basketball team!"

I don't know why I said that. I guess I was just nervous. And I had Judith on my mind and all that had happened that day, ending up with the *disaster* at basketball practice.

And so that was my wish. Of course I immediately felt like a complete jerk. I mean, of all the things to wish for in the world, why would anyone pick that?

But the woman didn't seem at all surprised.

She nodded, closing her eyes for a moment. The red ball glowed brighter, brighter, until the fiery red radiated around me. Then it quickly faded.

Clarissa thanked me again, turned, tucked the glass ball back in the purple bag, and began walking quickly away.

I breathed a sigh of relief. I was so glad she was gone!

I jumped on my bike, turned it around, and began pedalling furiously towards home.

A perfect end to a perfect day, I thought bitterly.

Trapped in the rain with a crazy woman.

And the wish?

I knew it was totally stupid.

I knew I'd never have to think about it again.

I found myself thinking about the wish at
dinner.

I couldn't get over the way the crystal ball had
glowed that strange red colour.

Mum was trying to get me to take another
helping of mashed potatoes, and I was refusing.
They were the kind from a box—you know, the
kind that didn't taste at all like real mashed
potatoes.

"Sam, you've got to eat more if you want to
grow big and strong," Mum said, holding the
bowl under my nose.

"Mum, I don't *want* to grow any more!" I
exclaimed. "I'm already taller than you are, and
I'm only twelve!"

"Please don't shout," Dad said, reaching for
the string beans. Tinned string beans. Mum gets
home from work late and doesn't have time to
make any *real* food.

"I was tall when I was twelve," Mum said

287

thoughtfully. She passed the potatoes to Dad.

"And then you shrank!" Ron exclaimed, sniggering. My older brother thinks he's so funny.

"I just meant I was tall for my age," Mum said.

"Well, I'm *too* tall for my age," I grumbled. "I'm too tall for *any* age!"

"In a few years you won't be saying that," Mum told me.

When she looked away, I reached under the table and fed some string beans to Punkin. Punkin is my dog, a little brown mutt. He'll eat *anything*.

"Are there more meatballs?" Dad asked. He knew there were. He just wanted Mum to get up and get them for him.

Which she did.

"How was basketball practice?" Dad asked me.

I made a face and gave a double thumbs-down.

"She's too tall for basketball," Ron mumbled with a mouth full of food.

"Basketball takes stamina," Dad said. Sometimes I can't figure out why Dad says half the things he says.

I mean, what am *I* supposed to say to that?

I suddenly thought of the crazy woman and the wish I had made. "Hey, Ron, want to shoot a few baskets after dinner?" I asked, poking my string beans around on the plate with my fork.

We have a hoop on the front of the garage and floodlights to light up the driveway. Ron and I play a little one-on-one sometimes after dinner. You know. To unwind before starting our homework.

Ron glanced out of the dining room window. "Has it stopped raining?"

"Yeah. It stopped," I told him. "About half an hour ago."

"It'll still be really wet," he said.

"A few puddles won't ruin your game," I told him, laughing.

Ron's a really good basketball player. He's a natural athlete. So of course he has almost no interest at all in playing with me. He'd rather stay up in his room reading a book. Any book.

"I've got a lot of homework," Ron said, pushing his black-framed glasses up on his nose.

"Just a few minutes," I pleaded. "Just a little shooting practice."

"Help your sister," Dad urged. "You can give her some pointers."

Ron reluctantly agreed. "But only for a few minutes." He glanced out the window again. "We're going to get soaked."

"I'll bring a towel," I said, grinning.

"Don't let Punkin out," Mum said. "He'll get his paws all wet and track mud on the floor."

"I can't believe we're doing this," Ron grumbled.

I knew it was stupid, but I had to see if my wish had come true.

Would I suddenly be a great basketball player?

Would I suddenly be able to outshoot Ron? To actually throw the basketball into the basket?

Would I be able to dribble without stumbling? To pass the ball in the direction I wanted? To catch the ball without it bouncing off my chest?

I kept scolding myself for even thinking about the wish.

It was so stupid. So completely stupid.

Just because a crazy woman offers to grant three wishes, I told myself, doesn't mean that you have to get all excited and think you're instantly going to turn into Michael Jordan!

Still, I couldn't wait to play with Ron.

Was I in for a big surprise!

Yes. I *was* in for a surprise.

My shooting was actually *worse*!

The first two times I tossed the ball at the hoop, I missed the garage entirely and had to go and chase the ball over the wet grass.

Ron laughed. "I see you've been practising!" he teased.

I gave him a hard shove in the stomach with the wet basketball. He deserved it. It wasn't funny.

I was so disappointed.

I told myself over and over that wishes don't come true, especially wishes granted by crazy women out wandering in the rain.

But I couldn't help but get my hopes up.

I mean, Judith and Anna and the other girls on the team were so mean to me. It would be absolutely terrific to come to the game against Jefferson Elementary tomorrow and suddenly be the star of the team.

291

The star. Ha-ha.

Ron dribbled the ball to the hoop and made an easy lay-up. He caught his own rebound and passed the ball to me.

It sailed through my hands and bounced down the driveway. I started running after it, slipped on the wet surface, and fell face down into a puddle.

Some star.

I'm playing *worse*! I told myself. Much worse! He helped me up. I brushed myself off.

"Remember, this was *your* idea!" he said.

With a determined cry, I grabbed the ball, darted past him, and dribbled furiously to the basket.

I had to make this basket. I *had* to!

But as I went up for my shot, Ron caught up with me. He leapt high, raised his arms, and batted the ball away.

"Aaaagggh!"

I let out a frustrated shout. *"I wish you were only a foot tall!"* I cried.

He laughed and ran after the ball.

But I felt a tremor of fear roll down my body.

What have I just done? I asked myself, staring into the darkness of the back garden, waiting for Ron to return with the ball. Have I just made my second wish?

I didn't mean to! I told myself, my heart thumping wildly in my chest. It was an accident.

It wasn't a real wish.

Have I just shrunk my brother down to a foot tall?

No. No. No. I repeated over and over, waiting for him to reappear.

The *first* wish hadn't come true. There was no reason to expect the second wish to come true.

I squinted into the heavy darkness of the back garden. "Ron—where are you?"

Then I gasped as he came scampering towards me over the grass—a foot tall—just as I had wished!

I froze like a statue. I felt as cold as stone.

Then, as the tiny figure emerged from the darkness, I started to laugh.

"Punkin!" I cried. "How did *you* get out?"

I was so happy to see him—so happy it wasn't a tiny Ron scampering over the grass—I picked up the little dog and hugged him tight.

Of course his paws got me covered with wet mud. But I didn't care.

Sam, you've just got to be cool, I scolded myself as Punkin struggled free. Your wish about Ron *couldn't* come true because Clarissa isn't here with her glowing red ball.

You've got to stop thinking about the three wishes, I told myself. It's just stupid. And you're making yourself crazy over them.

"What's going on? How'd *he* get out?" Ron cried, appearing from the side of the garage with the ball.

"Must've sneaked out," I replied with a shrug.

We played for a few more minutes. But it was cold and wet. And no fun at all, especially for me.

I didn't sink a single basket.

We finished with a foul shot competition, a short game of HORSE. Ron won easily. I was still on the O.

As we trotted back to the house, Ron patted me on the back. "Ever think of taking up tiddly-winks?" he teased. "Or maybe Snakes and Ladders?"

I uttered an unhappy wail. I had the sudden urge to tell him why I felt so disappointed, to tell him about the weird woman and the three wishes.

I hadn't told Mum or Dad about her, either. The whole story was just too stupid.

But I thought maybe my brother would find it funny. "I have to tell you about this afternoon," I said as we pulled off our wet trainers in the kitchen. "You won't believe what happened to me. I—"

"Later," he said, pulling off his wet socks and tucking them into his trainers. "I've got to get to that homework."

He disappeared up to his room.

I started walking to my room, but the phone rang. I picked it up after the first ring.

It was Cory, calling to ask how my basketball practice had gone after school.

"Great," I told him sarcastically. "Just great. I

295

was so fabulous, they're going to retire my number."

"You don't have a number," Cory reminded me. What a friend.

Judith tried to trip me in the cafeteria the next afternoon. But this time I managed to step over her outstretched trainer.

I made my way past Judith's table and found Cory nearly hidden in the corner near the waste baskets. He had already unwrapped his lunch and had a very unhappy expression on his face.

"Not toasted cheese again!" I exclaimed, dropping my brown paper lunchbag on to the table and pulling out the chair opposite him.

"Toasted cheese again," he muttered. "And look at it. I don't even think it's American cheese. I think my dad tried to slip in some cheddar."

I opened my chocolate-milk carton, then pulled my chair in closer. Across the room, some boys were laughing loudly, tossing a pink-haired Troll doll back and forth. It landed in someone's soup, and the table erupted in wild cheers.

As I picked up my sandwich, a shadow fell over the table. I realized that someone was standing behind me.

"Judith!" I cried, turning my head.

She sneered down at me. She was wearing a

296

green-and-white school sweater over dark green corduroys. "Are you coming to the game after school, Byrd?" she demanded coldly.

I put down the sandwich. "Yeah. Of course I'm coming," I replied, puzzled by the question.

"Too bad," she replied, frowning. "That means we don't have a chance of winning."

Judith's pal, Anna, suddenly appeared beside her. "Couldn't you get sick or something?" she asked me.

"Hey, give Sam a break!" Cory cried angrily.

"We really want to beat Jefferson," Anna said, ignoring him. She had dark red lipstick smeared on her chin. Anna wore more lipstick than all the other seventh-graders put together.

"I'll try my best," I replied through clenched teeth.

They both laughed as if I had made a joke. Then they walked off, shaking their heads.

If only my stupid wish would come true! I thought bitterly.

But of course I knew that it wouldn't.

I reckoned I was in for more embarrassment and humiliation at the game.

I had no idea just how surprising the game would turn out to be.

The game felt weird from the beginning.

The Jefferson team was mostly sixth-graders, and they were quite small. But they were well-coached. They really seemed to know where they were going. And they had a lot of energy and team spirit.

As they came trotting to the centre of the gym for the opening tip-off, my stomach was fluttery and I felt as if I weighed a thousand pounds.

I was really dreading this game. I knew I was going to mess it up. And I knew that Judith and Anna would be sure to let me know just how badly I messed it up, and how I let the team down.

So I was really shaky as the game started. And when, in the opening tip-off, the ball was slapped right to me, I grabbed it—and started dribbling towards the wrong basket!

Luckily, Anna grabbed me and turned me around before I could shoot a basket for Jefferson! But I could hear players on both teams laughing. And I glanced at the sidelines and saw that both coaches—Ellen and the Jefferson coach—were laughing, too.

I could feel my face turn beetroot-red. I wanted to stop right there and then and sink into a hole in the ground and never come out.

But—to my amazement—I still had the ball.

I tried to pass it to Judith. But I threw it too low, and a Jefferson girl stole it and started dribbling to our basket.

The game was ten seconds old, and I'd already made two mistakes!

I kept telling myself it was just a game, but it didn't really help. Every time I heard someone laugh I knew they were laughing at me, at how I'd started the game by running in the wrong direction.

When I looked up at the score for the first time, it was six-nil Jefferson.

The ball suddenly came sailing to me, seemingly from out of nowhere. I grabbed for it, but it slipped out of my hands. One of my team-mates took it, dribbled, then passed it back to me.

I took my first shot. It hit the backboard—a triumph for me—but didn't come near the basket. Jefferson took the rebound. A few seconds later, it was eight-nil.

I'm playing worse than ever! I moaned to myself. I could see Judith glaring angrily at me from across the floor.

I backed up, staying in the corner, away from the basket. I decided to try and keep out of the action as much as possible. Maybe that way I wouldn't embarrass myself quite so much.

After about five minutes into the first quarter, things started to get weird.

The score was twelve-two, Jefferson.

Judith threw the ball inwards. She meant to throw it to Anna. But Judith's toss was weak, and the ball bounced to a short, blonde-haired Jefferson player.

I saw Judith yawn as she ran after the girl.

A few seconds later, the ball was loose, bouncing near the centre of the court. Anna made a weak grab for it. But she seemed to be moving in slow motion, and the blonde Jefferson player snatched it from her hands.

Anna stood watching her, breathing hard, perspiration running down her forehead. I had to stop and stare. Anna looked *exhausted*—and we'd only been playing five minutes!

The Jefferson team dribbled all the way across the floor, passing the ball from girl to girl, as our players stood and watched.

"Let's go, Mustangs!" Judith cried, trying to rouse everyone. But I saw her yawn again as she walked to the sidelines to throw in the ball.

"Come on, girls! Hustle! Hustle!" Ellen was shouting from the sidelines, her hands cupped around her mouth. "Run, Judith—don't walk! Let's look *alive!*"

Judith sent another feeble throw on to the floor. It bounced away from a Jefferson player. I scooped it up and started to dribble it, running full speed.

Just outside the key, I stopped, turned, and looked for someone to pass it to.

But to my surprise, my team-mates were still far behind me, walking slowly, exhaustedly, in my direction.

As the Jefferson players swarmed around me, trying to take the ball away, I took a shot. It hit the rim of the basket—and bounced right back into my hands.

So I took another shot. And missed again.

Judith raised her hands slowly to catch the rebound. But the ball bounced right through her hands. She frowned in surprise, but didn't make a move to go after it.

I grabbed the ball, dribbled twice, nearly tripped over it—and shot.

To my amazement, the ball bounced on top of the hoop, landed on the rim, and then dropped through.

"Way to go, Sam!" I heard Ellen shout from the sidelines.

My team-mates uttered weak cheers. I watched them go after the Jefferson players, yawning and moving in slow motion, as if in some kind of trance.

301

"Pick it up! Pick it up!" Ellen was shouting encouragement.

But her words didn't seem to help.

Judith tripped and fell to her knees. As I stared in bewilderment, she didn't get up.

Anna was yawning loudly, walking towards the ball, not running.

My two other Mustang team-mates also seemed to be wandering hazily in slow motion, making lame attempts to defend our basket.

Jefferson scored easily.

Judith was still on her knees, her eyes half shut.

What on earth is happening? I wondered.

A long, shrill whistle broke into my thoughts. It took me a while to realize that Ellen had called time out.

"Mustangs—hustle up! Hustle up!" she shouted, motioning for us to cluster around her.

I quickly trotted over to Ellen. Turning back, I saw Judith, Anna, and the others trudging over slowly, yawning, pulling their bodies with great effort.

And as Ellen shouted for everyone to "hustle up," I watched them wearily approach. Then I realized to my amazement *that my wish had come true!*

"What's the matter, girls?" Ellen demanded as we huddled on the sidelines. She glanced from player to player, examining each one with concern.

Anna dropped down wearily on to the floor, her shoulders slumped. It looked like she could barely keep her eyes open.

Judith leaned her back against the gym's tiled wall. She was breathing hard, and beads of sweat rolled down her pale forehead.

"Let's get some energy," Ellen urged, clapping her hands. "I thought you girls were *pumped* for this game!"

"There's no air in here," one of the players complained.

"I feel so tired," another one said, yawning.

"Maybe we're coming down with something," Anna suggested from down on the floor.

"Do you feel sick, too?" Ellen asked me.

"No," I told her. "I feel okay."

Behind me, Judith groaned wearily and tried to push herself away from the wall.

The referee, a high school kid wearing a black-and-white-striped shirt about five sizes too big for him, blew his whistle. He signalled for us to get back out on the floor.

"I don't understand it," Ellen sighed, shaking her head. She helped pull Anna to her feet. "I don't understand it. I really don't."

I understood it.

I understood it perfectly.

My wish had come true. I couldn't believe it! That strange woman really did have some kind of magical powers. And she had granted my wish.

Only not quite the way I had imagined.

I remembered my words so clearly. I had wished to be the strongest player on the basketball team. That meant I wanted the woman to make me a stronger, better player.

Instead, she had made everyone else *weaker!*

I was the same clumsy player I'd always been. I still couldn't dribble, pass, or shoot.

But *I was the strongest player in the team!*

How could I have been such a fool? I scolded myself angrily as I trotted back to the centre of the gym floor. Wishes *never* turn out the way you want them to.

When I reached the centre court, I turned back and saw Judith, Anna, and the others trudging on to the floor. Their shoulders were slumped, and they dragged their trainers over the floor as they walked.

I have to admit I enjoyed it just a little.

I mean, I felt perfectly fine. And they looked so weak and pitiful.

Judith and Anna really deserve it, I told myself. I tried not to grin as they slumped into their places. But maybe I was smiling just a little.

The referee blew his whistle and called for a jump ball to start things off. Judith and a Jefferson player faced each other at the centre circle.

The referee tossed the ball up. The Jefferson girl jumped high. Judith made a real effort. I could see the strain on her face.

But her feet didn't even leave the floor.

The Jefferson player batted the ball to one of her team-mates, and they headed down the floor with it.

I chased after them, running at full speed. But the rest of my team could only walk.

Jefferson scored with an easy lay-up.

"Come on, Judith—we can catch them!" I shouted, clapping my hands cheerfully.

Judith glared dully at me. Her green eyes looked faded, sort of washed out.

"Pick it up! Pick it up! Let's go, Mustangs!" I cheered energetically.

I was really enjoying rubbing it in.

Judith could barely bounce the ball inwards. I picked it up and dribbled all the way down the floor. Under the basket, one of the Jefferson players bumped me from behind as I tried to shoot.

Two foul shots for me.

It took my slow-motion team-mates forever to make their way down the floor to line up.

Of course, I missed both of my foul shots.

But I didn't care.

"Let's go, Mustangs!" I shouted, clapping my hands energetically. "Defence! Defence!"

Suddenly I had become both a player *and* a cheerleader. I was really enjoying being the best player on the team.

Watching Judith and Anna droop around and drag their bodies back and forth like tired losers was the biggest hoot! It was so wonderful!

We lost the game by twenty-four points.

Judith, Anna, and the others looked glad it was over. I started to trot to the changing room to get changed, a big smile on my face.

I was nearly changed by the time my team-mates dragged into the room. Judith walked up to me and leaned against my locker. She eyed me suspiciously.

"How come *you're* so peppy?" she demanded.

I shrugged. "I don't know," I told her. "I feel okay. Same as ever."

Sweat was pouring down Judith's forehead. Her red hair was matted wetly against her head.

"What's going on here, Byrd?" she demanded, yawning. "I don't get it."

"Maybe you're coming down with the 'flu or something," I said, trying to hide how much I was enjoying this.

This was *great!*

"Ohhh, I'm so tired," Anna moaned, coming up behind Judith.

"I'm sure you'll both feel better tomorrow," I chirped.

"There's something weird going on here," Judith murmured weakly. She tried to stare hard at me, but her eyes were too tired to focus.

"See you tomorrow!" I said brightly, picking up my stuff and heading out. "Feel better, girls!"

I stopped outside the changing room door.

They *will* feel better tomorrow, I assured myself. They'll be back to normal tomorrow.

They won't stay like this—right?

Right??

The next day, the bad news hit me like a ton of bricks.

Judith and Anna weren't in school the next morning.

I stared at their empty seats as I made my way to my seat in the front row. I kept turning back, searching for them. But the bell rang, and they weren't there.

Absent. Both absent.

I wondered if the other girls on the team were absent, too.

I felt a cold shiver run down my back.

Were they still weak and tired? Too weak and tired to come to school?

I had a frightening thought: What if they *never* returned to normal? What if the magic *never* wore off?

Then I had an even more frightening thought: What if Judith and Anna and the others got weaker and weaker? What if they kept getting weaker until they *died*—and it was all my fault?

All my fault. All my fault.

I felt cold all over. My stomach felt as if I'd swallowed a rock. I had never felt so guilty, so horribly guilty, in all my life.

I tried to force these thoughts from my mind, but I couldn't.

I couldn't stop thinking that they might *die* because of my careless wish.

I'll be a *murderer*, I told myself with a shudder. A *murderer*.

Sharon, our teacher, was standing right in front of me, talking about something. I couldn't hear a word she said. I kept turning in my seat, staring back at the two empty chairs.

Judith and Anna. *What have I done to you?*

At lunch, I told the whole story to Cory.

Of course he just laughed at me. He had a mouthful of toasted cheese and nearly choked.

"Do you believe in the Easter Bunny, too?" he asked.

But I was in no mood for jokes. I was really upset. I stared down at my uneaten lunch, and felt sick.

"Please take me seriously, Cory," I begged. "I know it sounds stupid—"

"You mean you're for *real?*" he asked, his eyes studying my face. "I thought you were kidding, Sam. I thought this was a story for creative writing or something."

I shook my head. "Listen, Cory—if you had

309

been at the girls' basketball game yesterday afternoon, you'd know I'm not kidding," I said, leaning across the table and whispering. "They were dragging around as if they were sleepwalking," I told him. "It was so eerie!"

I was so upset, my shoulders started to shake. I covered my eyes to keep myself from crying.

"Okay . . . let's think about this," Cory said softly, his funny, crooked smile fading to a thoughtful frown. Finally, he had decided to take me seriously.

"I've been thinking and thinking about it all morning," I told him, still trying to force back the tears. "What if I'm a *murderer*, Cory? What if they really *die?*"

"Sam, please," he said, still frowning, his dark brown eyes studying mine. "Judith and Anna are probably not even sick. You're probably making this all up in your mind. They're probably perfectly okay."

"No way," I muttered glumly.

"Oh. I know!" Cory's face brightened. "We can ask Audrey."

"Audrey?" Audrey was the school nurse. It took me a while to figure out what Cory was thinking. But I finally did.

He was right. When you were going to be absent, your parents had to phone Audrey in the morning and tell her why. Most likely, Audrey would be able to tell us why Judith and Anna were not in school today.

I jumped up, nearly knocking my chair over. "Great idea, Cory!" I exclaimed. I started running through the cafeteria towards the door.

"Wait! I'll come with you!" Cory called, hurrying to catch up.

Our trainers pounded against the hard floor as we made our way along the long corridor to the nurse's office. We found Audrey locking the door.

She is a short, sort of chunky woman, about forty or so, I suppose, with bleached-blonde hair pinned up into a bun on top of her head. She always wears baggy jeans and shaggy sweaters, never a nurse's uniform.

"Lunch-time," she said, seeing us stop beside her. "What do they have today? I'm starving."

"Audrey, can you tell us why Judith and Anna aren't in school today?" I demanded breathlessly, ignoring her question.

"Huh?" I was talking so fast, so excitedly, I don't think she understood me.

"Judith Bellwood and Anna Frost?" I repeated, my heart pounding. "Why aren't they in school today?"

I saw surprise in Audrey's pale grey eyes. Then she lowered her gaze.

"Judith and Anna, they're gone," she said sadly.

I stared at her. My mouth dropped open in horror. "They're gone?"

"They're gone for at least a week," Audrey said. She bent to lock the office door.

"They—*what?*" I squeaked.

She had trouble pulling the key from the lock. "They went to the doctor," she repeated. "Their mums called this morning. They're very sick. Both girls have the 'flu or something. They felt weak. Too weak to come to school."

I breathed a sigh of relief. I was glad Audrey had been concentrating on the door lock, so she hadn't seen the horrified look on my face.

Audrey hurried off down the corridor. As soon as she was out of sight, I slumped against the wall. "At least they're not *dead*," I moaned. "She scared me to death!"

Cory shook his head. "Audrey scared me, too," he confessed. "See? Judith and Anna just have the 'flu. I'm sure the doctors—"

"They don't have the 'flu," I insisted. "They're weak because of my wish."

"Call them later," he suggested. "You'll see. They'll probably be much better."

"I can't wait till later," I said in a trembling voice. "I have to do something, Cory. I have to do something to keep them from getting weaker and weaker until they shrivel up and die!"

"Calm down, Sam—"

I started pacing back and forth in front of him. Some kids came hurrying by, on their way to their lockers. Someone called to me, but I didn't reply.

"We've got to get to class," Cory said. "I think you're getting all weird over nothing, Sam. If you wait till tomorrow—"

"She said I had three wishes!" I exclaimed, not hearing a word Cory was saying. "I only used one."

"Sam—" Cory shook his head disapprovingly.

"I've got to find her!" I decided. "I've got to find that strange woman. Don't you see? I can wish to have the first wish undone. She *said* I get three wishes. So my second wish can to be erase the first!"

This idea was starting to make me feel a lot better.

But then Cory brought me back down into my gloom with one question:

"How are you going to find her, Sam?"

I thought about Cory's question all afternoon. I barely heard a word anyone said to me.

We had a vocab test near the end of the day. I stared at the words as if they were in Martian!

After a while, I heard Lisa, my teacher, calling my name. She was standing right in front of me, but I don't think I heard her until her fifth or sixth try.

"Are you okay, Samantha?" she asked, leaning over me. I knew she was wondering why I hadn't started my test.

"I feel a little sick," I replied quietly. "I'll be okay."

I'll be okay as soon as I find that weird woman and get her to erase her spell!

But where will I find her? I wondered. Where?

After school, I reported to the gym for basketball practice. Everyone on my team was absent, so practice was cancelled.

Absent because of me . . .

I trudged upstairs to my locker and retrieved my jacket. As I slammed the door and locked it, I had an idea.

The woods. Jeffers' Woods.

That's where I found Clarissa.

I'll bet I can find her there again.

Maybe it's her secret meeting place, I thought. Maybe she'll be waiting for me there.

Of *course* she will! I told myself, giving myself a pep talk. Why did it take me so long to think of this? It made perfect sense.

Humming to myself, I started jogging to the door. The corridor was nearly empty.

I stopped when I saw a familiar figure in the doorway. "Mum!"

"Hi, Sam." She waved to me, even though I was standing right in front of her. She had a red-and-white wool cap pulled over her short blonde hair, and was wearing the tattered red ski jacket she always wears.

She hadn't been skiing in years. But she liked dressing like a ski bum.

"Mum—what are you doing here?" I cried, not meaning it to sound as unfriendly as it did. I was eager to get to my bike and ride to Jeffers' Woods. I didn't need *her* here!

"You didn't forget about your appointment with Mr Stone?" she asked, waving her car keys in her hand.

315

"The orthodontist? Today?" I cried. "I *can't!*"

"You have to," she replied sternly, tugging the arm of my jacket. "You know how hard it is to get in to see Mr Stone."

"But I don't *want* a brace!" I cried, realizing I was sounding a little shrill, a little babyish.

"Maybe you won't need one," Mum said, pulling me towards the door. "Maybe you can get by with just a retainer. We'll do whatever Mr Stone says."

"But, Mum—I—I—" I searched my mind desperately for an excuse. "I can't go with you. I have my bike here!" I cried desperately.

"Go and get it. We'll put it in the boot," she replied without blinking.

I had no choice. I had to go with her. Sighing loudly, I pushed open the door and hurried past her towards the bike racks.

I found out I'm going to be wearing a brace for at least the next six months. I had another appointment with Mr Stone to have one put on the next week.

I suppose I should have been upset about it. But it was hard to think about a brace with Judith, Anna, and the other girls on my mind.

I kept picturing them wasting away, getting

thinner and thinner, weaker and weaker. I kept seeing this terrifying image in my mind. I was in the gym, dribbling the ball back and forth, faster and faster. And Judith, Anna, and the others were lying flat on their backs on the benches, trying to watch, but too weak to hold their heads up.

That night after dinner, I was feeling so guilty, I phoned Judith to see how she was feeling. I think it was the first time in my life I had ever called her.

Mrs Bellwood answered. She sounded tired and tense. "Who is this?" she asked.

I had a sudden impulse to hang up. But I told her, "It's Samantha Byrd. I'm a friend from school."

Some friend.

"I don't think Judith can come to the phone," she replied. "She's just so weak."

"Did the doctor say what—?" I started.

"I'll ask Judith if she wants to talk," Mrs Bellwood interrupted. I could hear Judith's little brother shouting something in the background. And I could hear cartoon music coming from their TV. "Don't stay on too long," she instructed.

"Hello?" Judith answered in a faint, little-girl voice.

"Oh. Hi, Judith. It's me. Sam," I said, trying not to sound nervous.

317

"Sam?" Again the faint voice, nearly a whisper.

"Sam Byrd," I stammered. "I—I just wondered how you were feeling."

"Sam, did you cast a spell on us?" Judith asked.

I gasped. *How did she know?*

318

"Judith—what do you mean?" I spluttered.

"All the girls are sick except for you," Judith replied. "Anna is sick. And so is Arlene. And Krista."

"Yes, but that doesn't mean—" I started.

"So I think you cast a spell on us," Judith interrupted.

Was she joking? I couldn't tell.

"I just hope you feel better," I mumbled awkwardly. I could hear Mrs Bellwood in the background telling Judith she should get off the phone.

So I said goodbye and hung up. I was grateful it was a short conversation. But I couldn't decide if Judith was joking or not about my casting a spell.

Her voice was really weak. She sounded so weary and lifeless.

I felt angry that she had accused me, joke or no joke. That was so typical of Judith. Finding a way to make me angry even when I was ringing her to be nice.

But I also felt guilty. Whether Judith had guessed it or not, I *had* cast a spell on her and the others.

And now I had to find a way to have the spell removed.

The next morning, two seats in my class were empty again. Judith and Anna were both absent.

At lunch, I asked Cory if he wanted to come with me after school to go searching for the strange woman.

"No way!" he cried, shaking his head. "She'll probably turn me into a frog or something!"

"Cory—can't you take this seriously?" I screamed. Several kids turned to look.

"Give me a break," Cory muttered, blushing under his Orlando Magic cap.

"Okay, I'm sorry," I told him. "I'm really stressed out—d'ya see?"

He still refused to keep me company. He made up a lame excuse about having to help his mother clean the cellar.

Who cleans a cellar in the middle of winter?

Cory pretended he didn't believe my story about the woman and the three wishes. But I had the feeling that maybe he was a little afraid.

I was afraid, too. Afraid I wouldn't find her.

After school, I jumped on my bike and began pedalling towards Jeffers' Woods.

It was a grey, blustery day. Enormous, dark clouds rolled rapidly over the sky, threatening rain, maybe snow.

It's a lot like the day I ran into Clarissa, I thought. For some reason, that fact encouraged me.

Some kids in my class waved to me and called out. But I rode past them, leaning over the handlebars, shifting gears to pick up speed.

A few minutes later, Montrose Avenue curved away from the houses that lined both sides, and the bare trees of the woods came into view.

The tall trees formed a dark wall, darker than the charcoal sky above.

"She's got to be here, got to be here," I repeated in rhythm with my pedalling feet.

Got to be here, got to be here.

My heart nearly leapt out of my chest when I saw her, huddled low at the edge of the road.

Waiting for me.

"Hi!" I called out. "Hi! It's me!"

Why didn't she answer?

As I pedalled closer, my heart pounding happily, I saw that she had her back turned to me.

She had changed her outfit. She was wearing a purple wool beret, and a long black coat down nearly to her ankles.

I screeched my bike to a halt a few feet behind her, my tyres skidding over the pebbly road. "I need to make another wish!" I called breathlessly.

She turned, and I gasped.

I stared into a face full of freckles, a young-looking face framed by short, curly blonde hair.

"I'm sorry. What did you say?" she asked, narrowing her eyes at me, her expression bewildered.

"I—I'm sorry," I stammered, feeling my face turn hot. "I—I thought you were someone else."

It was a different woman.

I felt so embarrassed, I just wanted to die!

Behind her, I saw two blonde-haired kids tossing a frisbee back and forth at the edge of the woods. "Tommy—don't throw it so hard. Your sister can't catch it!" the woman instructed.

Then she turned back to me. "What did you say about wishes? Are you lost?" she asked, studying my face with concern.

I knew I was still blushing, but I couldn't help it. "No. I thought you were—" I started.

"Tommy—go and chase it yourself!" she shouted to her little boy. The two kids started squabbling. She hurried over to settle it.

"Sorry I bothered you," I called. "'Bye." I turned my bike around and started pedalling rapidly towards home.

I was embarrassed that I'd said such a stupid thing to a total stranger. But mainly I was disappointed.

I really had expected the strange woman to be there.

Where else could she be? I asked myself.

I remembered that I had shown her the way to Madison Road. Maybe, I decided, I will get lucky and run into her there.

It was a long shot. But I was desperate.

I turned my bike around and made my way to Madison Road. The wind had picked up, and my face began to feel cold and raw. I was riding against the wind, and the sharp cold was making my eyes water.

Even through the blur, I could see that the woman was not hanging around on Madison Road, waiting for me to show up.

Two mangy brown dogs trotted side by side across the street, their heads bowed against the wind. They were the only living creatures I saw.

I rode slowly back and forth a few times, my eyes searching the rambling old houses of the neighbourhood.

A complete waste of time.

I was really frozen. My ears and nose tingled with numbness. My watering eyes sent cold tears rolling down my cheeks.

"Give up, Sam," I instructed myself aloud.

The sky darkened. The storm clouds hovered low above the shivering trees.

Feeling miserable and defeated, I turned and headed for home. I was pedalling furiously down the centre of the street, trying to keep my bike upright in the gusting wind.

I stopped when Judith's house came into view. It was a long, low, redwood ranch-style house, set back from the street on a wide, sloping front lawn.

Maybe I'll stop for a minute and see how Judith is doing, I decided.

It'll give me a chance to get warm, too, I

thought. I reached up a hand and felt my nose. Absolutely numb.

Shivering, I rode up the driveway and lowered my bike to the ground. Then, trying to rub some feeling into my poor nose, I jogged up the path and rang the bell.

Mrs Bellwood seemed very surprised to see a visitor. I told her who I was and that I just happened to be riding by. "How is Judith feeling?" I asked, shivering.

"About the same," she replied with a worried sigh. She had Judith's green eyes, but her hair was nearly grey.

She led me into the corridor, which felt nice and warm. The house smelled of roasting chicken. I suddenly realized I was hungry.

"Judith! You have a visitor!" Mrs Bellwood shouted up the stairs.

I heard a weak reply, but couldn't make out the words.

"Go on up," Judith's mother said, putting a hand on the shoulder of my coat. "You look so cold," she added, shaking her head. "Be careful, dear. You don't want to get sick, too."

I climbed the stairs and found Judith's room at the end of the corridor. I hesitated at the doorway and peered in.

The room was dimly lit. I could see Judith lying in bed, on top of the quilt, her head propped up on several pillows. Books and magazines and a couple of school notebooks were scattered over the bed. But Judith wasn't reading. She was just staring straight ahead.

"Stork?" she cried, seeing me in the doorway.

I entered the room, forcing a smile to my face. "How are you feeling?" I asked softly.

"What are *you* doing here?" she asked coldly. Her voice was hoarse.

"I—I was riding my bike, and—" I stammered, staying by the door. I was startled by her anger.

"Riding your bike? In this cold?" With great effort, she pulled herself up to a sitting position. Leaning against the headboard, she glared at me suspiciously.

"I just wondered how you were," I muttered.

"Why don't you just fly away, Byrd!" she growled nastily.

"Huh?"

"You *are* a witch—aren't you?" she accused.

I couldn't believe she was saying these things. I was stunned. Shocked! It was no joke. I could see clearly that she was serious!

"You *did* cast a spell on us. I know it!"

"Judith—please," I cried. "What are you *saying*?"

"We did a study on witches in social sciences last year," she said in her hoarse voice. "We studied spells and things."

"That's crazy!" I insisted.

"You were jealous of me, Sam. Of me and Anna and everyone else," Judith accused.

"So?" I cried angrily.

"So, all of a sudden all the girls on the team feel weak and sick. Except for you, Sam. You feel fine—right?"

"Judith listen to me—" I pleaded.

"You're a witch, Sam!" she screamed, her weak voice breaking. She started to cough.

"Judith, you're talking like a crazy person," I insisted. "I'm not a witch. How could I be a witch? I'm sorry you're sick. Really, I am. But—"

"You're a witch! You're a witch!" Judith chanted, her voice a shrill whisper. "I've talked to all the girls. They all agree. You're a witch. A witch!"

I was so furious, I thought I'd explode. I had my hands clenched into tight fists. My head was throbbing.

Judith had been talking to all the other girls, spreading this story that I was a witch. How could she do such a crazy thing?

"A witch! You're a witch!" she continued to chant.

I was so upset. I really lost it. *"Judith—"* I shrieked. *"I—I never would have done it to you if you hadn't been so horrible to me!"*

I realized immediately that I'd made a terrible mistake.

I had just admitted to her that I *was* responsible for her being sick.

I had just blurted out that I *was* a witch!

But I was so furious, I didn't care.

"I *knew* it!" Judith croaked in her hoarse voice, her green eyes glowing excitedly, pointing an accusing finger at me.

"What's going on here? What's all the shouting?" Judith's mother appeared in the room, her eyes flashing back and forth between Judith and me.

"She's a witch! A witch!" Judith screamed.

"Judith—your voice! Stop!" Mrs Bellwood cried, running to the bed. She turned back to me. "I think Judith is delirious. She—she's saying such crazy things. Please don't pay attention. She—"

"She's a witch! She admitted it! She's a witch!" Judith shrieked.

"Judith—please. Please, you have to calm down. You have to save your strength," Mrs Bellwood pleaded.

"I'm sorry. I'll go now," I said sharply.

I darted out of the room, ran down the stairs, and out of the house as fast as I could.

"*A witch! A witch!*" Judith's hoarse chant followed me out.

I was so angry, so hurt, so humiliated, I felt I was about to explode. "I wish Judith would *disappear!*" I screamed. "I really do!"

328

"Very well. That shall be your second wish," said a voice behind me.

I spun around to see the strange woman standing at the side of the house, her long, black hair fluttering behind her in the gusting wind. She held the glowing red ball high. Her eyes glowed as red as the ball.

"I shall cancel your first wish," she said in her shaky, old lady's voice. "And I shall grant your second."

"No—wait!" I cried.

The woman smiled and pulled her shawl over her head.

"Wait! I didn't mean it!" I cried, running towards her. "I didn't know you were there. Wait—OW!"

My foot caught on a loose stone in the path, and I stumbled. I hit my knees hard. The pain shot up through my entire body.

When I looked up, she was gone.

After dinner, Ron agreed to play basketball at the back of the house. But it was too cold and windy. A light snow had started to fall.

We settled for ping-pong in the basement.

Ping-pong games in our basement are always difficult. For one thing, the ceiling is so low, the ball is always hitting it and bouncing crazily away. Also, Punkin has a bad habit of chasing after the ball and biting holes in it.

Ping-pong is the only sport I'm good at. I have a really tricky serve, and I'm good at slamming the ball down my opponent's throat. I can usually beat Ron two games out of three.

But tonight he could see my heart wasn't in it.

"What's up?" he asked as we batted the ball softly back and forth. His dark eyes peered into mine from behind his black-framed glasses.

I decided I *had* to tell him about Clarissa, and her red crystal ball, and the three wishes. I was so desperate to tell someone.

"I helped this strange woman a few days ago," I blurted out. "And she granted me three wishes. I made a wish, and now all the girls on my basketball team are going to die!"

Ron dropped his bat on to the table. His mouth dropped open. "What an amazing coincidence!" he cried.

"Huh?" I gaped at him.

"I met my fairy godmother yesterday!" Ron exclaimed. "She promised to make me the richest person in the world, and she's going to give me a solid gold Mercedes with a swimming pool in the back!"

He burst out laughing. He thinks he's so funny.

"Aaaaagh!" I let out an angry, frustrated groan. Then I threw my bat at him and ran upstairs to my room.

I slammed the bedroom door behind me and began to pace back and forth, my arms crossed tightly in front of me.

I kept telling myself that I had to calm down, that it wasn't good to be this stressed out. But of course, telling yourself to calm down doesn't do any good. It only makes you more tense.

I decided I had to do something to occupy my mind, to keep myself from thinking about Judith, and Clarissa, and the new wish I had accidentally made.

My second wish.

"It's not fair!" I cried aloud, still pacing.

After all, I didn't know I was making a second wish. That woman tricked me! She appeared out of nowhere—and tricked me!

I stopped in front of my mirror and fiddled with my hair. I have very fine, light blonde hair. It's so fine, there isn't much I can do with it. I usually tie it in a ponytail on the right side of my head. It's a style I saw on a model that looked a little like me in *Seventeen*.

Just to keep my hands busy, I tried doing something else with my hair. Studying myself in the mirror, I tried sweeping it straight back. Then I tried parting it in the middle and letting it fall over my ears. It looked really pathetic.

The activity wasn't helping. It wasn't taking my mind off Judith at all. I pulled it back into the same old ponytail. Then I brushed it for a while, tossed down the brush with a sigh, and returned to pacing.

My big question, of course, was: had my wish come true?

Had I caused Judith to disappear?

As much as I hated Judith, I certainly didn't want to be responsible for making her disappear forever.

With a loud moan, I threw myself down on to my bed. What should I do? I asked myself. I *had* to know if the wish had come true.

I decided to phone her house.

I wouldn't talk to her. I'd just call her house and see if she was still around.

I wouldn't even tell them who was calling.

I looked up Judith's number in the school directory. I didn't know it by heart. I had only called it once before.

My hand was shaking as I reached for the phone on my desk. I punched in her phone number.

It took me three tries. I kept making mistakes.

I was really scared. I felt as if my stomach was tied in a knot and my heart had jumped up into my throat.

The phone rang. One ring. Two rings. Three rings.

Had she disappeared?

Four rings.

No answer.

"She's gone," I murmured aloud, a chill running down my back.

Before the fifth ring could begin, I heard a clicking sound. Someone had picked up the receiver.

"Hello?"

Judith!

"Hello? Who *is* this?" she demanded.

I slammed the receiver down.

My heart was pounding. My hands were ice-cold.

I breathed a sigh of relief. Judith was there. She was definitely there. She hadn't vanished from the face of the earth.

And, I realized her voice had returned to normal.

She didn't sound hoarse or weak. She sounded as nasty as ever.

334

What did this mean? I jumped to my feet and began to pace back and forth, trying to figure it all out.

Of course, I *couldn't* figure it out.

I only knew that the second wish hadn't been granted.

Feeling a little relieved, I went to bed and quickly fell into a heavy, dreamless sleep.

I opened one eye, then the other. Pale morning sunlight was shining through my bedroom window. With a sleepy groan, I pushed down the covers and started to sit up.

My eye went to the clock above my desk and I gasped.

Nearly ten past eight?

I rubbed my eyes and looked again. Yes. Ten past eight.

"Huh?" I cried, trying to clear the sleep from my voice. Mum wakes me every morning at seven so I can get to school by eight-thirty.

What happened?

There was no way I'd be on time now.

"Hey—Mum!" I shouted. "Mum!" I jumped out of bed. My long legs got tangled up in the covers, and I nearly fell over.

Great way to start the day—with a typical Samantha idiotic move!

"Hey, Mum—" I shouted out of the bedroom door. "What happened? I'm late!"

Not hearing a reply, I pulled off my nightshirt and quickly searched through the wardrobe for some clean clothes to wear. Today was Friday, laundry day. So I was down to the bottom of the pile.

"Hey, Mum? Ron? Anybody up?"

Dad leaves the house for work every morning at seven. Usually I hear him moving around. This morning I hadn't heard a sound.

I pulled on a pair of faded jeans and a pale green sweater. Then I brushed my hair, staring at my still-sleepy face in the mirror.

"Anybody up?" I shouted. "How come no one woke me today? It's not a holiday—is it?"

I listened carefully as I tugged on my Doc Martens.

No radio on down in the kitchen. How weird, I thought. Mum has that radio tuned to the all-news station every morning. We fight about it every morning. She wants news, and I want music.

But today I couldn't hear a sound down there. What's going on?

"Hey—I'm going to have to skip breakfast!" I shouted down the stairs. "I'm late."

No reply.

I took one last look in the mirror, brushed a strand of hair off my forehead, and hurried out into the corridor.

My brother's room is next door to mine. His door was closed.

Uh-oh, Ron, I thought. Did you sleep late, too?

I pounded on the door. "Ron? Ron, are you awake?"

Silence.

"Ron?" I pushed open the door. His room was dark, except for the pale light from the window. The bed was made.

Had Ron already left? Why had he made his bed? It would be the first time in his life he ever had!

"Hey, Mum!" Confused, I hurried down the stairs. Halfway down, I stumbled and nearly fell. Idiot Move Number Two. Pretty good for so early in the morning.

"What's going on down here? Is it the week-end? Did I sleep through Friday?"

The kitchen was empty. No Mum. No Ron. No breakfast.

Did they have to go to somewhere early? I checked the fridge for a note.

Nothing.

Puzzled, I glanced at the clock. Nearly eight-thirty. I was already late for school.

Why didn't anyone wake me up? Why were they all gone so early in the morning?

I pinched myself. I really did. I thought maybe I was dreaming.

But no such luck.

"Hey—anyone?" I called. My voice rang through the empty house.

I ran to the corridor cupboard to get my coat. I had to get to school. I was sure this mystery would be cleared up later.

I quickly pulled on my coat and ran upstairs for my backpack. My stomach was grumbling and growling. I was used to having at least a glass of fruit juice and a bowl of cereal for breakfast.

Oh, well, I thought, I'll buy an extra big lunch.

A few seconds later, I headed out of the front door and around to the side to the garage to get my bike. I pulled up the garage door—and stopped.

I froze, staring into the garage.

My dad's car. It was still in the garage.

He hadn't left for work.

So where was everyone?

338

Back in my house I phoned my dad's office. The phone rang and rang, and no one answered.

I checked the kitchen again for a message from Mum or Dad. But I couldn't find a thing.

Glancing at the kitchen clock, I saw that I was already twenty minutes late for school. I needed a late excuse note, but there was no one to write it for me.

I hurried back outside to get my bike. Better late than never, I thought. I wasn't exactly frightened. I was just puzzled.

I'll call Mum or Dad at lunchtime and find out where everyone went this morning, I told myself. As I pedalled to school, I began to feel a little angry. They could've at least told me they were leaving early!

There were no cars on the street, and no kids on bikes. I guessed that everyone was already at school or work or wherever people go in the morning. I got to school in record time.

339

Leaving my bike in the bike rack, I adjusted my backpack on my shoulders and ran into the school. The corridors were dark and empty. My footsteps echoed loudly on the hard floor.

I dropped my coat into my locker. When I slammed the locker door, it sounded like an explosion in the empty corridor.

The corridors are sort of creepy when they're this empty, I thought. I jogged to my classroom, which was just a few doors down from my locker.

"My mum forgot to wake me, so I overslept."

That was the excuse I'd planned to give Sharon as soon as I entered. I mean, it wasn't just an excuse. It was the truth.

But I never got to tell Sharon my reason for being late.

I pulled open the door to the classroom—and stared in shock.

Empty. The room was empty.

No kids. No Sharon.

The lights hadn't been turned on. And yesterday's work was still on the blackboard.

Weird, I thought.

But I didn't know then how weird things were going to get.

I froze for a moment, staring into the empty, dark room. Then I decided that everyone must be at an assembly in the main hall.

I turned quickly and made my way to the main

hall at the front of the school, jogging down the empty corridor.

The door to the staff room was open. I peered in and was surprised to find it empty, too. Maybe all the teachers are at the assembly, I thought.

A few seconds later, I pulled open the double doors to the hall.

And peered into the darkness.

The room was silent and empty.

I pushed the doors shut and began to run down the corridor, stopping to look into every room.

It didn't take me long to realize that I was the only person in the building. No kids. No teachers. I even checked the cleaners' room downstairs. No cleaners.

Is it Sunday? Is it a holiday?

I tried to figure out where everyone had gone, but I couldn't.

Feeling the first stirrings of panic in my chest, I dropped a quarter into the payphone next to the head teacher's office and called home.

I let it ring at least ten times. Still no one home.

"Where *is* everyone?" I shouted down the empty corridor. The only reply came from my echoing voice.

"Can *anybody* hear me?" I shouted, cupping my hands around my mouth. Silence.

I suddenly felt very frightened. I had to get out of the creepy school building. I grabbed my coat

341

and started to run. I didn't even bother to close the locker door.

Carrying my coat over my shoulder, I ran outside, to the bike rack. My bike was the only bike parked there. I scolded myself for not noticing that when I arrived.

I pulled on my coat, arranged my backpack, and started for home. Again, I saw no cars on the street. No people.

"This is so *weird!*" I cried aloud.

My legs suddenly felt heavy, as if something was weighing them down. I knew it was my panic. My heart was pounding. I kept searching desperately for someone—anyone—on the street.

Halfway home, I turned around and headed my bike to town. The small shopping district was just a few streets north of school.

I rode into the middle of the street. There was no reason not to. No cars or trucks appeared in either direction.

The bank came into view, followed by the grocery shop. As I pedalled as hard as I could, I noticed all the other shops that lined both sides of Montrose Avenue.

All dark and empty.

Not a soul in town. Not a single person in any shop.

No one.

I braked the bike in front of Farber's Hardware Store and jumped off. The bike fell on to its side. I stepped on to the pavement and listened. The only sound was the banging of a shutter being blown by the wind above the barber's shop.

"Hello!" I called at the top of my voice. "Hellllooooo!"

I started running frantically from shop to shop, pressing my face against the windows, peering inside, searching desperately for another human being.

Back and forth. I covered both sides of the street, my fear growing heavier inside me with each step. With each dark shop.

"Hellooooo! Helllooooo! Can anybody hear me?"

But I knew it was a waste of my voice.

Standing in the middle of the street, staring at the dark shop and empty pavements, I knew that I was alone.

Alone in the world.

I suddenly realized my second wish had been granted.

Judith had disappeared. *And everyone else had disappeared with her.*

Everyone.

My mum and dad. My brother, Ron. Everyone.

Would I ever see them again?

I slumped down on to the cement step in front of the barber's shop and hugged myself, trying to stop my body from trembling.

Now what? I wondered miserably. *Now what?*

343

I don't know how long I sat there on the step, hugging myself, my head lowered, my mind in a total, spinning panic. I would have sat there forever, listening to the banging shutter, listening to the wind blow through the deserted street—if my stomach hadn't started to growl and grumble.

I stood up, suddenly remembering that I had missed my breakfast.

"Sam, you're all alone in the world. How can you think about eating?" I asked myself aloud.

Somehow it was comforting to hear a human voice, even though it was my own.

"I'm staaaaarving!" I shouted.

I listened for a response. It was really stupid, but I refused to give up hope.

"This is all Judith's fault," I muttered, picking my bike up from the street.

I rode home through the empty streets, my eyes searching the deserted gardens and houses.

344

As I passed the Carters' house on the corner of my street, I expected their little white terrier to come yapping after my bike the way he always did.

But there weren't even any dogs left in my world. Not even my poor little Punkin.

There was just me. Samantha Byrd. The last person on earth.

As soon as I got home, I rushed into the kitchen and made myself a peanut butter sandwich. Gobbling it down, I stared at the open peanut butter jar. It was nearly empty.

"How am I going to feed myself?" I wondered aloud. "What do I do when the food runs out?"

I started to fill a glass with orange juice. But I hesitated, and filled it up only halfway.

Do I rob the grocery shop? I asked myself. Do I just *take* the food I need?

Is it really robbing if there's no one there? If there's no one *anywhere?*

Does it matter? Does *anything* matter?

"How can I take care of myself? I'm only twelve!" I shouted.

For the first time, I felt the urge to cry. But I jammed another hunk of peanut butter sandwich into my mouth and forced the urge away.

Instead, I turned my thoughts to Judith, and my unhappiness and fear quickly gave way to anger.

If Judith hadn't made fun of me, hadn't tried

to embarrass me, if Judith hadn't constantly sneered at me and said, "Byrd, why don't you just fly away!" and all the other horrible things she'd said to me, then I never would have made any wishes about her, and I wouldn't be all alone now.

"I hate you, Judith!" I screamed.

I jammed the last section of sandwich into my mouth—but I didn't chew.

I froze. And listened.

I heard something.

Footsteps. Someone walking in the living room.

I swallowed the sandwich section whole, and went tearing into the living room. "Mum? Dad?"

Were they back? Were they really back?

No.

I stopped in the living room doorway when I saw Clarissa. She was standing in the centre of the room, her black hair reflecting the light from the front window, a pleased smile on her face.

Her bright red shawl was draped loosely over her shoulders. She wore a long black jumper over a white, high-collared blouse.

"You!" I cried breathlessly. "How did you get in?"

She shrugged. Her smile grew wider.

"Why did you *do* this to me?" I shrieked, my anger bursting out of me. "*How* could you do this to me?" I demanded, gesturing at the empty room, the empty house.

"I didn't," she replied quietly.

She walked to the window. In the bright

347

afternoon sunlight, her skin appeared pale and wrinkled. She looked so old.

"But—but—" I spluttered, too furious to speak.

"You did it," she said, her smile fading. "You made the wish. I granted it."

"I didn't wish for my family to disappear!" I screamed, striding into the room, my hands clenched into tight fists. "I didn't wish for *everyone in the world* to disappear! *You* did that! *You!*"

"You wished for Judith Bellwood to disappear," Clarissa said, adjusting the shawl on her shoulders. "I granted the wish as best as I knew how."

"No. You tricked me," I insisted angrily.

She sniggered. "Magic is often unpredictable," she said. "I thought you would not be happy with your last wish. That is why I have returned. You have one more wish. Would you like to make it now?"

"Yes!" I exclaimed. "I want my family back. I want all the people back. I—"

"Be careful," she warned, pulling the red glass ball from the purple bag. "Think carefully before you make your final wish. I am trying to repay your kindness to me. I do not want you to be unhappy with the results of your wish."

I started to reply, but stopped.

She was right. I had to be careful.

I had to make the right wish this time. And I had to say it the right way.

"Take your time," she urged softly. "Since this is your final wish, it shall be permanent. Be very careful."

I stared into her eyes as they turned from black to red, reflecting the red glow of the ball in her hand, and I thought as hard as I could.

What should I wish for?

The light from the living room window faded as clouds rolled over the sun. As the light dimmed, the old woman's face darkened. Deep black ruts formed beneath her eyes. Lines creased her forehead. She seemed to sag into the shadows.

"Here is my wish," I said in a trembling voice. I spoke slowly, carefully. I wanted to consider each word. I didn't want to slip up this time.

I didn't want to give her a chance to trick me.

"I am listening," she whispered, her face completely covered by shadow now. Except for her eyes, glowing as red as fire.

I cleared my throat. I took a deep breath.

"Here is my wish," I repeated carefully. "I wish for everything to return to normal. I want *everything* to be exactly the way it was—but—"

I hesitated.

Should I finish this part of it?

Yes! I told myself.

"I want everything to be the way it was—but I

want Judith to think that I'm the greatest person who ever lived!"

"I will grant your third wish," she said, raising the glass ball high. "Your second wish will be cancelled. Time will back up to this morning. Goodbye, Samantha."

"Goodbye," I said.

I was swallowed up by the radiating red glow. When it faded, Clarissa had vanished.

"Sam! Sam—rise and shine!"

My mother's voice floated up to my room from downstairs.

I sat straight up in bed, instantly awake. "Mum!" I cried happily.

I remembered everything. I remembered waking up in an empty house, in an empty world. And I remembered my third wish.

But time had gone back to this morning. I glanced at the clock. Seven. Mum was waking me up at the usual time.

"Mum!" I leapt out of bed, ran downstairs in my nightshirt, and joyfully threw my arms around her, hugging her tight. "Mum!"

"Sam? Are you okay?" She stepped back, a startled expression on her face. "Are you running a fever?"

"Good morning!" I cried happily, hugging Punkin, who seemed just as startled. "Is Dad still at home?" I was so eager to see him, too,

351

to know that he was back.

"He left a few minutes ago," Mum said, still examining me suspiciously with her eyes.

"Oh, Mum!" I exclaimed. I couldn't conceal my happiness. I hugged her again.

"Whoa!" I heard Ron enter the kitchen behind us.

I turned to see him staring at me, his eyes narrowed in disbelief behind his glasses. I ran over and hugged him, too.

"Mum—what did you put in her orange juice?" he demanded, struggling to back away from me. "Yuck! Let *go* of me!"

Mum shrugged. "Don't ever ask me to explain your sister," she replied dryly. She turned to the kitchen cabinets. "Go and get dressed, Sam. You don't want to be late."

"What a beautiful morning!" I exclaimed.

"Yeah. Beautiful," Ron repeated, yawning. "You must have had some terrific dreams or something, Sam."

I laughed and hurried upstairs to get dressed.

I couldn't wait to get to school. I couldn't wait to see my friends, to see the halls filled once again with talking, laughing faces.

Pedalling my bike as hard as I could, I grinned every time a car passed. I loved seeing people again. I waved at Mrs Miller across the street, bending to pick up her morning newspaper.

I didn't even mind it when the Carters' terrier

came chasing after my bike, barking his high-pitched yips and nipping at my ankles.

"Good dog!" I cried gleefully.

Everything is normal, I told myself. Everything is wonderfully normal.

I opened the front door to school to the sound of crashing locker doors and shouting kids. "Great!" I cried aloud.

A sixth-grader came tearing around the corner and bumped right into me, practically knocking me over as I made my way to the locker. I didn't cry out angrily. I just smiled.

I was *so happy* to be back in school, back in my crowded, noisy school.

Unable to stop grinning, I unlocked my locker and pulled open the door. I called out a cheerful greeting to some friends in the corridor.

I even said good morning to Mrs Reynolds, our head teacher!

"Hey—Stork!" a seventh-grade boy called to me. He made a funny face, then disappeared around the corner.

I didn't care. I didn't care what anyone called me. The sound of so many voices was so wonderful!

As I started to take my coat off, I saw Judith and Anna arrive.

They were busy chatting, both talking at once. But Judith stopped when she saw me.

"Hi, Judith," I called warily. I wondered what

Judith would be like now. Would she treat me any differently? Would she be nicer to me?

Would she remember how much she and I used to hate each other?

Would she be any different at all?

Judith gave Anna a little wave and came hurrying over to me. "Morning, Sam," she said, and smiled.

Then she pulled off her wool ski cap—and I gasped.

"Judith—your hair!" I cried in astonishment.

"Do you like it?" she asked, staring at me eagerly.

She had cut it shorter like mine and had tied a ponytail on the side—just like mine!

"I—I suppose so . . ." I stammered.

She breathed a sigh of relief and smiled at me. "Oh, I'm so glad you like it, Sam!" she cried gratefully. "It looks just like yours, doesn't it? Or did I cut it too short? Do you think it should be longer?" She studied my hair. "I think yours might be longer."

"No. No. It's . . . great, Judith," I told her, backing towards my locker.

"Of course, it's not as good as yours," Judith continued, staring at my ponytail. "My hair just isn't as pretty as yours. It isn't as fine, and the colour is too dark."

I don't believe this! I thought.

"It looks good," I said softly.

I pulled my coat off and hung it inside my locker. Then I bent down to pick up my backpack.

"Let me carry that," Judith insisted, She grabbed it out of my hands. "Really. I don't mind, Sam."

I started to protest, but Anna interrupted. "What are you doing?" she asked Judith, flashing me a cold glance. "Let's get to the next lesson."

"You go without me," Judith replied. "I want to carry Sam's backpack for her."

"Huh?" Anna's mouth dropped open. "Are you completely losing it, Judith?" she demanded.

Judith ignored her question and turned back to me. "I love that T-shirt, Sam. It's ribbed, isn't it? Did you get it at the Gap? That's where I got mine. Look. I'm wearing one just like yours."

I goggled in surprise. Sure enough, Judith was wearing the same style T-shirt, only hers was grey and mine was pale blue.

"Judith—what's your problem?" Anna asked, applying a twentieth layer of bright orange lipstick on her lips. "And what did you do to your hair?" she cried, suddenly noticing the new style.

"Doesn't it look just like Sam's?" Judith asked her, flipping the ponytail with one hand.

Anna rolled her eyes. "Judith, have you turned psycho or something?"

"Give me a break, Anna," Judith replied. "I'd like to talk to Sam—okay?"

"Huh?" Anna knocked on Judith's head, as if knocking on a door. "Anyone home?"

"See you later, okay?" Judith said impatiently.

Anna sighed, then walked away angrily.

Judith turned back to me. "Can I ask you a favour?"

"Yeah. Sure," I replied. "What kind of favour?"

She hoisted my backpack over her left shoulder. Her own backpack hung on her right shoulder. "Would you help me work on my foul shot at practice this afternoon?"

I wasn't sure I had heard Judith correctly. I stared at her, my mouth hanging open.

"Would you?" she pleaded. "I'd really like to try shooting fouls your way. You know. Under-handed. I bet I'd have a lot more control shooting them under-handed, the way you do."

This was too much! *Too much!*

As I stared at Judith, I saw absolute *worship* in her eyes!

She was the best foul shooter on the team. And here she was begging me to show her how to shoot the clumsy way I did it!

"Yeah. Okay. I'll try to help you," I told her.

"Oh, thank you, Sam!" she cried gratefully. "You're such a friend! And do you think I could borrow your social studies notes later? Mine are such a mess."

"Well . . ." I said thoughtfully. My notes were so bad, even I couldn't make them out.

"I'll copy them and get them right back to you. Promise," Judith said breathlessly. I think the weight of two backpacks was starting to get to her.

"Okay. You can borrow them," I told her.

We started walking to class. Several kids stopped to stare at Judith, lugging two backpacks on her shoulders.

"Where did you get your Doc Martens?" she asked as we entered the room. "I want to get a pair just like yours."

What a laugh! I thought, very pleased with myself. This is such a laugh!

The change in Judith was simply hilarious. It was all I could do not to burst out laughing.

Little did I know then that my laughter would quickly turn to horror.

It started to get really embarrassing. Judith wouldn't leave me alone.

She hung around me wherever I went. When I got up to sharpen my pencil, she followed me and sharpened hers.

My throat got dry during a spelling test, and I asked Lisa if I could run out to the water fountain to get a drink. As I was bending over the fountain, I turned and saw Judith right behind me. "My throat is dry like yours," she explained, faking a cough.

Later, during reading hour, Lisa had to separate Judith and me because Judith wouldn't stop talking.

At lunch, I took my usual place on the opposite side of the table from Cory. I had just started telling him about Judith's new attitude—when she appeared at our table.

"Could you move down a seat?" she asked the kid sitting next to me. "I want to sit next to Sam."

The kid moved, and Judith dropped her lunch tray on to the table and took her seat. "Would you like to swap lunches?" she asked me. "Yours looks so much better than mine."

I was holding a mashed-up tunafish sandwich. "This?" I asked, waving it. Half the tunafish fell out of the soggy bread.

"Yum!" Judith exclaimed. "Want my pizza, Sam? Here. Take it." She slid her tray in front of me. "You bring great lunches. I wish my mum packed lunches like yours."

I could see Cory staring at me, his eyes wide with disbelief.

I really couldn't believe it, either. All Judith wanted from the world was to be exactly like me!

A few tables away, near the wall, Anna sat by herself. She looked really glum. I saw her glance over to our table, frowning. Then she quickly lowered her eyes to her lunch.

After lunch, Judith followed me to my locker. She helped me pull out my books and notebooks and asked if she could carry my backpack.

At first, I thought this was all really funny. But then I started to get annoyed. And embarrassed.

I saw that kids were laughing at us. Two boys from my class followed us down the corridor, sniggering. I heard other kids talking about Judith and me in the corridor. They stopped when Judith and I walked by, but I saw amused smirks on their faces.

She's making me look like a complete idiot! I realized.

The whole school is laughing at us!

"Are you getting a brace?" Judith asked me as we made our way back to the classroom. "Someone told me you were getting a brace."

"Yeah. I'm getting one," I grumbled, rolling my eyes.

"Great!" Judith declared. "Then I want to get one, too!"

After school I hurried to the gym, expecting to have basketball practice. In all the excitement over the wishes, I had forgotten that we had an actual game that afternoon.

The girls' team from Edgemont Middle School was already on the floor, warming up by shooting lay-ups. Most of their shots were dropping in. They were big, tough-looking girls. We had heard that they were a really good team—and they looked it.

I changed quickly and hurried out of the locker room. My team-mates were huddled around Ellen for last-minute instructions. As I jogged over to them, I crossed my fingers on both hands and prayed that I wouldn't make too big a fool of myself in the game.

Judith grinned at me as I joined the huddle. Then she practically embarrassed me out of my

Reeboks by shouting, "Here she is! Here comes our star!"

Anna and the others laughed, of course.

But then their smiles quickly faded when Judith interrupted Ellen to announce, "Before the game starts, I think we should name Sam team captain."

"You're joking!" Anna cried.

A few girls laughed. Ellen stared at me, bewildered.

"Our best player should be captain," Judith continued in all seriousness. "So it should be Sam, not me. All in favour, raise your hand."

Judith shot her hand up in the air, but no one else did.

"What's your problem?" Anna asked her nastily. "What are you trying to do, Judith—ruin our team?"

Judith and Anna got into an angry shouting match over that, and Ellen had to pull them apart.

Ellen stared at Judith as if she had lost her mind or something. Then she said, "Let's worry about who's captain later. Let's just go out and play a good game, okay?"

The game was a disaster.

Judith copied everything I did.

If I tried to dribble, and tripped over my feet, Judith would dribble and trip. If I threw a bad pass that was intercepted by the other team,

Judith would throw a bad pass.

When I missed an easy lay-up under the basket, Judith did the same thing, deliberately missing the next time she had the ball.

It was one disaster after another—doubled because of Judith copying me!

And the whole time, she kept clapping and shouting, cheering me on. "Way to go, Sam! Nice try, Sam! You're the *best*, Sam!"

It was so obnoxious!

And I could see the girls on the Edgemont team sniggering at us, and laughing out loud when Judith fell head-first into the benches just because I had done it a few plays before.

Anna and the other players on my team weren't laughing. Their expressions were glum and angry.

"You're deliberately messing up!" Anna accused Judith about halfway through the game.

"I am *not!*" Judith replied shrilly.

"Why are you copying that clumsy ox?" I heard Anna demand.

Judith grabbed her and knocked her down, and they began wrestling angrily on the floor, screaming and tearing at each other furiously.

It took Ellen and the referee to stop the fight. Both girls were given a harsh lecture about sportsmanship and sent to the changing room.

Ellen made me sit down on the bench. I was

glad. I really didn't feel like playing any more.

As I watched the rest of the game, I couldn't concentrate on it at all. I kept thinking about my third and final wish, and how I'd blown it again.

To my dismay, I realized that having Judith worship me was much worse than having her hate me! At least when she hated me, she left me alone!

I had made three wishes, and each of them had turned into a nightmare. Now I was stuck with Judith following me around, hanging on to my every word, constantly praising everything I did, fawning over me like a lovesick puppy—and, mainly, being an unbelievable pest!

I actually longed for the days when she had made fun of me in front of the whole class, when she had followed after me, calling, "Byrd, why don't you fly away! Why don't you fly away, Byrd!"

But what could I do? My three wishes were up.

Was I going to be stuck with Judith for the rest of my life?

We lost the game by fifteen or sixteen points. I didn't pay much attention to the score. I just wanted to get out of there.

But when I trudged into the changing room to change, Judith was waiting for me. She handed me a towel. "Good game!" she cried, slapping me a high-five.

"Huh?" I could only gape at her.

"Can we study together after dinner?" she asked with pleading eyes. "Please? You could help me with my algebra. You're so much better at it than I am. You're a real genius when it comes to algebra."

Luckily, I had to go with my parents to visit my aunt after dinner. That gave me a good excuse not to study with Judith.

But what would be my excuse the next night? And the next, and the next?

My aunt wasn't feeling well, and the purpose of our visit was to cheer her up. I'm afraid I didn't do a very good job. I barely said a word.

I couldn't stop thinking about Judith.

What could I do about her? I could get angry and tell her to leave me alone. But I knew that wouldn't help. I had wished for her to think I was the greatest person who ever lived. Now Judith was under an enchantment, under the power of the Crystal Woman's spell.

Telling her to go away wouldn't discourage her in the least.

Could I just ignore her? That wouldn't be easy since she was constantly in my shadow, asking me a million questions, begging to wait on me like a servant.

What could I do? *What?*

I thought about it all the way home. Even my parents noticed I was distracted.

"What's the problem, Sam?" my mother

365

demanded as we drove home.

"Oh, nothing," I lied. "Just thinking about schoolwork."

When we got home, there were four phone messages on the answering machine for me, all from Judith.

My mother stared at me, curious. "That's funny. I don't remember you being friends with her before," she said.

"Yeah. She's in my class," I told her. I didn't want to explain. I knew I *couldn't* explain.

I hurried up to my bedroom. I was totally exhausted, from all the worrying, I guess. I got changed into a nightshirt, clicked off the light, and climbed into bed.

For a while, I lay staring up at the ceiling, watching shadows of the tree outside my window weave back and forth. I tried to clear my mind, tried to picture fluffy white sheep leaping over fluffy white clouds.

I was just drifting off to sleep when I heard the floorboards creak.

Opening my eyes wide, I saw a black shadow move against the darkness of my cupboard.

I uttered a choked cry as I realized that someone was in my room.

Before I could move, a hot, dry hand grabbed me by the arm.

I tried to scream, but the hand slid up over my mouth.

I—I'm going to choke! I thought, frozen in panic. I can't breathe!

"Shh—don't scream!" my attacker whispered.

The light clicked on.

The hand left my mouth.

"Judith!" I rasped, my voice catching in my throat.

She smiled at me, her green eyes flashing with excitement, and raised a finger to her lips. "Sshhh."

"Judith—what are you *doing* here?" I managed to cry, finding my voice. My heart was still pounding so hard, I could barely breathe. "How did you get in?"

"Your back door was unlocked," she whispered. "I hid in the cupboard to wait for you. I think I fell asleep for a little while."

"But why?" I demanded angrily. I pulled

myself up and lowered my feet to the floor. "What do you want?"

Her smile faded. Her mouth formed a pout. "You said we could study together," she said in a little-girl voice. "So I waited for you, Sam."

This was the last straw. "Get out!" I cried.

I started to say more, but a knock on my door startled me into silence.

"Sam—are you okay?" my dad called in. "Are you talking to someone?"

"No. I'm fine, Dad," I said.

"You're not on the phone, are you?" he asked suspiciously. "You know you're not supposed to call people this late."

"No. I'm going to sleep now," I told him.

I waited till I heard his footsteps on the stairs. Then I turned back to Judith. "You have to go home," I whispered. "As soon as the coast is clear—"

"But why?" she demanded, hurt. "You said we'd study our algebra."

"I did not!" I cried. "Anyway, it's too late. You have to go home. Your parents must be going nuts worrying about you, Judith."

She shook her head. "I sneaked out. They think I'm asleep in bed." She smiled. "But that's so great of you to worry about my parents, Sam. You really are the most considerate girl I know."

Her stupid compliment made me even angrier. I was so furious, I wanted to tear her apart with my bare hands.

"I *love* your room," she gushed, glancing around quickly. "Did you choose all the posters yourself?"

I sighed in total exasperation.

"Judith, I just want you to go home—now," I snarled slowly, one word at a time, so that maybe she would hear me.

"Can we study together tomorrow?" she pleaded. "I really need your help, Sam."

"Maybe," I replied. "But you can't sneak into my house any more, and—"

"You're so clever," Judith gushed. "Where did you get that nightshirt? The stripes are terrific. I wish I had one like it."

Motioning for her to be silent, I crept out into the hall. All the lights had been turned off. My parents had gone to bed.

Tugging Judith by the hand, I led the way downstairs, tiptoeing silently, taking it one step at a time. Then I practically shoved her out of the front door and swung it closed with a soft click behind her.

I stood in the dark corridor, panting hard, my mind racing.

What can I do? What can I do? What can I do?

It took me hours to get to sleep. And when I

369

finally drifted off, I dreamed about Judith.

"You look tired, dear," my mum said at breakfast.

"I didn't sleep very well," I confessed.

When I headed out of the front door to go to school, Judith was waiting for me by the driveway.

She smiled at me and waved cheerily. "I thought we could walk to school this morning," she chirped. "But if you want to ride your bike, I'll be happy to run alongside."

"No!" I shrieked. "No! Please—*no!*"

I completely lost it. I just couldn't stand it any more.

I dropped my backpack and started to run. I didn't know where I was running. And I didn't care.

I just knew I had to run away from her.

"Sam—wait! Wait for me!"

I turned to see her chasing after me. "No—please! Go away! *Go away!*" I screamed.

But I could see her pick up speed, her trainers thudding against the pavement, starting to catch up.

I turned into someone's garden and ran behind a hedge, trying to lose her.

I didn't really know what I was doing. I had no plan, no destination. I just had to *run!*

I was running through back gardens now,

across driveways, behind garages.

And Judith followed, running at full speed, her short ponytail bobbing as she ran. "Sam—wait! Sam!" she called breathlessly.

Suddenly I was running through woods, a thick tangle of trees and tall weeds. I weaved through them, first this way, then that, jumping over fallen branches, plunging through thick piles of dead, brown leaves.

I've got to lose her! I told myself. I've got to get away!

But then I stumbled over an upraised tree root and fell, sprawling face down on the carpet of dead leaves.

Typical clumsy move.

And a second later, Judith was standing over me.

26

I glanced up from the ground—and saw to my shock that it wasn't Judith.

Clarissa hovered over me, her red shawl tight around her shoulders, her black eyes staring intently.

"You!" I cried angrily, and started to scramble to my feet.

"You are unhappy," she said softly, frowning.

"Your wishes have ruined my life!" I cried, furiously brushing dead leaves off the front of my sweater.

"I don't want you to be unhappy," she replied. "I was trying to repay your kindness."

"I wish I'd never met you!" I cried angrily.

"Very well." She raised the round red crystal ball in one hand. As she raised it, her dark eyes began to glow, the same scarlet colours as the crystal. "I will cancel your third wish. Make one final wish. Since you are so unhappy, I shall grant you one more."

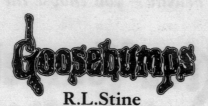

R.L.Stine

Reader beware, you're in for a scare!
These terrifying tales will send shivers up your spine:

Reader beware – you choose the scare!

Give Yourself Goosebumps

A scary new series from R.L. Stine – where *you* decide what happens!

Give Yourself Goosebumps 1:
Escape From the Carnival of Horrors

Late one night you and your friends decide to visit the annual carnival. It's not open yet, but you sneak in anyway. *Big* mistake. Because sneaking out again might not be so easy…

Pick one ending and you'll all ride on the deadly Doom Slide till the end of time. Select another, and you'll be trapped in a freak show … for ever. So be careful how you choose your rides … and your endings!

If you like animals, then you'll love
Hippo Animal Stories!

Thunderfoot
Deborah van der Beek
When Mel finds the enormous, neglected horse
Thunderfoot, she doesn't know it will change her
life for ever...

Vanilla Fudge
Deborah van der Beek
When Lizzie and Hannah fall in love with the same dog,
neither of them will give up without a fight...

A Foxcub Named Freedom
Brenda Jobling
An injured vixen nudges her young son away from her.
She can sense danger and cares nothing for herself – only
for her son's freedom...

Pirate the Seal
Brenda Jobling
Ryan's always been lonely – but then he meets Pirate
and at last he has a real friend...

Animal Rescue
Bette Paul
Can Tessa help save the badgers of Delves Wood
from destruction?

HIPPO FANTASY

Lose yourself in a whole new world, a world where anything is possible – from wizards and dragons, to time travel and new civilizations... Gripping, thrilling, scary and funny by turns, these Hippo Fantasy titles will hold you captivated to the very last page.

The Night of Wishes
Michael Ende

Malcolm and the Cloud-Stealer
Douglas Hill

The Crystal Keeper
James Jauncey

The Wednesday Wizard
Sherryl Jordan

Ratspell
Paddy Mounter

Rowan of Rin
Rowan and the Travellers
Emily Rodda

The Practical Princess
Jay Williams